Sarah

Sarah

a novella

Mike Trial

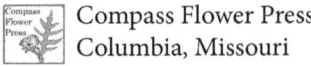

Compass Flower Press
Columbia, Missouri

Published by Compass Flower Press
Columbia, Missouri
compassflowerpress.com

Cover painting by Jane Mudd. Used with permission.

Book design by Yolanda Ciolli.
Author photo © Yolanda Ciolli. Used with permission.

Library of Congress Control Number: 2020906696

ISBN: 978-1-951960-01-8 Trade Paper
ISBN: 978-1-951960-02-5 E-book

Chapter 1

By eight o'clock in the morning, I'd gotten rid of Alex and spent a frenetic ten minutes clearing off empty bottles and full ashtrays from last night. Then exhaustion caught up with me, and I slumped in my only chair. I'd gotten about two hours sleep last night.

Outside the grimy window, bits of snow drifted down from a gray sky. I poured myself a shot of Bushmills, lit a Marlboro, and tried to let my mind relax from the jittering high I had been on since the reception last night when Ellis had told me that one of my paintings had sold.

And it had been one of what Ellis called my "serious" paintings. Ellis, who runs Tempus Gallery, had agreed to show four of my works—big, extravagant representations of faces: melds of people I'd seen on the subway, on the street, in bars. Not happy people, but distracted, suspicious, angry people, simmering with frustration, caught up in their internal worlds.

I was proud of the work, maybe a bit too proud, but I knew they were good—the best work I'd done so far. When he'd taken me aside at the reception last night and showed me a red stick-on dot he was about to put on the title card of one of my pieces, my mind had begun to race. It had still not stopped.

"Who bought it?" I had asked Ellis, but he only grinned at me and shook his head. I suddenly felt the need to be cautious about how I acted; I needed to be nonchalant about this sale. The buyer might still be in the room. He might change his mind if he saw me acting like a twit, jumping and clapping with joy. That is not done in NYC. You need to be always cool, assertive, but keeping an edge of mystery.

"I can't tell you," Ellis told me. "The buyer wants to remain anonymous, but no matter. You're on your way, Sarah. More than one person has asked about your stuff tonight. I wouldn't be surprised if I don't get another one sold very soon." He frowned at me. "But don't get big-headed about it. I know most of the people in here tonight. I know those that never buy, and those that sometimes buy. And I know what the buyers will buy. Besides, the person who bought your piece may have no interest in it at all, except as an investment if they think you'll start selling enough later to bring the prices up."

"A speculator bought my painting?"

"I'm not going to tell you. I've seen several talented

painters get all wound up about the fact that people are only buying their stuff to try to make a profit. That thought gets stuck in their head and the quality of their work drops. I don't want that to happen to you."

"Just tell me if you think the person who bought my piece is a speculator or an art lover, that's all. I don't need to know their name."

The party was getting noisy. Ellis shouted in my ear, "Like every artist I've known, your misperceptions about the art trade interfere with you doing good work, so quit asking me these questions. Your job is to paint great paintings."

I nodded. "That's cool." A woman pulled Ellis away, and I wandered through the crowd to my stuff, amazed at the titles Ellis had made up for my paintings, and even more amazed at the prices he'd put on them: low five figures. The child in me was astounded. Someone would pay that much money for something that came out of my head. Since my junior year at NYU, painting had become an obsession. I could no more stop putting paint on canvas than I could stop breathing.

I drifted over to the bar. "Bushmills neat." But then I found myself fidgeting again, not knowing where to stand, who to talk to, what to do. Chiding myself for being so nervous—for being afraid I'd make some sort of mistake and my first sale would be canceled. I downed the whiskey and walked four blocks down Essex Street to Club 70, where I was pretty sure I'd find Alex.

Alex and I had been seeing each other for a few months. He had little interest in art, but he knew how to listen to me talking about it.

He was there at the bar, talking to some guy whose name I'd forgotten. "Hey Alex," I said.

"Sarah." We touched cheeks. "Thought you had a gallery gig to do this evening."

"I did." Alex nodded. His friend was eyeing me rather speculatively. "We've met before," I told him. "I'm Sarah; can't remember your name."

He didn't smile. "Max. Yeah, hello." He downed his drink and set the empty glass down hard on the bar. "I need to get going." And he was gone.

"Your friend Max having a tough day?" I asked, sitting down on his barstool.

Alex shrugged. "Nothing serious. Money problems. So tell me, how did the reception go?"

So I told him, my excitement growing, and one drink led to another and eventually led us to bed in my apartment.

The next morning, after Alex had left, I wandered around the apartment, mixed some paint, and started touching up a painting I had on the easel. But I found I was making it worse, not better.

"Time to stop messing with this one." I cleaned up, pulled on a jacket, and went outside.

I needed to get out of my apartment for a while, so I took the subway to the Museum of Modern Art, which opens early. I went up to the fifth floor and started working my way down from level to level, just like I had in my student days at NYU. A couple hours of that calmed me down. I stopped somewhere for lunch at a crowded counter, then back to Essex Street, Tempus Gallery. It was just opening.

The sullen girl who works for Ellis was at the desk doing nothing. She ignored me as I walked to Ellis's tiny office in the back. I found Ellis looking through boxes of files.

"Hi, Ellis," I said cheerily. "I was wondering if you'd take some more…"

He straightened up. "Way too soon. Don't start in on me to show more of your work just because you sold one. And by the way, you don't get your money until thirty days after I take down the show. Read your contract."

"I'm fine with that," I said. I pulled my cigarettes out then shoved them back in my purse. Ellis went back to rummaging through boxes of paper—his so-called "files." I'd hate to see what his tax records looked like.

"See that paper napkin on my desk," he said without looking up. "You need to phone that woman. Name's Astrid. I don't know her last name." I picked up the red-and-white cocktail napkin and looked at the phone number.

"What does she want?"

"I've no idea, but I'll tell you this—she owns 404 Gallery over on Eldridge Street, and I won't have you selling your stuff through her. Your contract stipulates Tempus has an exclusive right to all your work for one year from date of signing."

"Take it easy, Ellis, I'm not going to be making any deals behind your back."

On the phone Astrid sounded pleasant, had a strong Italian accent, and went straight to the point without saying what the point was. "I would like to speak to you. Better to speak in person, don't you agree?"

We agreed to meet for drinks at four o'clock at Club 70, which is not quite the rathole you might think, though it does cater to artists.

Astrid turned out to be a pleasant-looking woman with thick blonde hair, northern Italian features, and a wide face not unlike the actress Monica Vitti. She was well dressed and affable, but I couldn't help thinking she might turn out to be a bit of an airhead. I had been in her gallery; I'd been in all the galleries in our part of town, the lower east side. It was very nicely appointed, and the art, mostly by Italian artists I didn't know, was good but not exceptional.

We chatted about this and that for a time. She mentioned her gallery, and I complimented her on it and the art I'd seen in it. I deduced she must be well-to-do—or someone in her family was—since she mentioned she, or they, had another gallery in Milan. Astrid tended to use a lot of unconnected pronouns, so

I couldn't always tell which "he" she was talking about: an artist, the owner, or one of her assistant managers.

She congratulated me on my sale last night (word travels fast), and I was about to tell her about my contract with Tempus Gallery when she said, "I don't want to ask you to show your art in my gallery; that would not be fair to Ellis. I know Ellis," she continued. "I wish him to succeed, to be happy. He's not a very happy person, I think?"

"I agree. He is too serious."

That was an understatement. Since I'd known him I think I'd heard him laugh twice.

"What I would like for you to do," Astrid continued, after a demure sip of Campari and soda, "is to evaluate some art I might like to show. Tell me if you think it is commercially viable."

"I'm flattered you ask. I'm only a year out of art school…only sold my first piece last night. And Ellis has endlessly lectured me on how artists should stay out of the art trade and focus only on creating art. Art and the art business are two different worlds."

She smiled. "Ellis is right, of course. He worries a young artist like you will be influenced by fads and trends and your own work will deteriorate. But at the same time, a young artist may have a feel for what other artists their own age are producing, whether it has real value or is…a bit superficial, you know?" She smiled again. "And Ellis has told me you are a bit different from the other young artists. I say this not to flatter you, but because talking to you now I believe it is true. You are more…organized. Maybe that is the right word. I will pay you for your time, of course."

I finished my Bushmills and stopped myself from ordering another one. "Well, I'd be happy to give you my opinion, for what it's worth. How soon do you need this evaluation?"

She spread her hands in a movie-style Italian gesture then pushed her unfinished Campari and soda aside. "Next week."

I looked at my empty glass. I had two paintings partly done and wanted badly to get them done, but on the other hand I could tell that until the elation of my first sale wore off, I would have trouble concentrating.

But I'd spent a lot of mental energy on those two paintings, both figure studies. I'd spent a lot of money on them too. In New York, figure study sessions were expensive and exclusive. Somebody had to vouch for you to be accepted into one.

On the other hand, Astrid's studio was not that far from my apartment, and I shouldn't pass up a chance to work with a gallery owner like her, with influence from here to Milan.

"I'll be happy to evaluate your paintings," I told her, with a smile I hoped wasn't too false. "How many are there?"

Astrid smiled again. She seemed to smile a lot, but her smiles felt genuine. "There are forty of them. I will be asking you to keep your information confidential. I flatter myself that I know something about the salability of art, but it is useful to have other opinions."

"Other artists will also be evaluating these paintings?"

"Yes, of course, but separately. I'll not share the names of your colleagues, or your notes to me about the paintings. This is strictly for me."

I could spend a few hours one afternoon next week looking through forty paintings and a few more hours writing down my thoughts for a "small honorarium." Actually, it would be good practice for me. I could go back to the art books and my notes from my classes and refresh myself on what I'd been taught. I wouldn't be able to guarantee commercial salability, but I should be able to furnish a thoughtful analysis. Even hardened professional art dealers can't guarantee commercial, much less critical, success. Nobody can.

"When can I start?"

Astrid smiled. "I think you must be an only child. You are very decisive. I mean that as a compliment."

Surprised, I said, "No I have a younger sister, Lisa. Four years younger than me."

"You are the eldest." Astrid smiled warmly. "I am also the eldest in my family. I think it is a good thing. I apologize for being so…what's the word?"

"Inquisitive?"

"Yes." She laid out money for the drinks. "And to answer your question, you can start right away."

As we made our way to the door, Astrid said over her shoulder, "The paintings are not at our gallery on Eldridge Street. They're at Galerie Etienne, a gallery I own, my family owns, in Milan."

I followed her out onto the crowded sidewalk where we stood against the glass windows of the bar out of the way of the people passing by.

"Milan, Italy?"

"Yes," Astrid said complacently. "We will pay your expenses, of course."

I was nodding. "I can travel," I heard myself say.

"Is next Thursday too soon? There is a flight leaving JFK at ten p.m."

"That will be fine," I replied.

"You will be met at the airport in Milan; your hotel is arranged." She handed me her business card. The 404 Gallery here in New York on one side and Galerie Etienne, her gallery in Milan, on the other side.

Astrid gave me a quick hug, which I did not return.

"The ticket will be waiting for you at the United Airlines counter." She waved and was gone.

I walked the four blocks back to my apartment, trying to let the cold wind clear my head.

Italy. Next week.

Chapter 2

My first day in Milan, jet-lagged and disoriented, I still managed to get a lot done. The flight from New York arrived in Milan at six a.m. I took a taxi to my hotel and tried to sleep until noon without much luck, then I made my way to Astrid's gallery. The paintings Astrid wanted me to evaluate were pretty good, but not very good. Would any of them sell? Probably. If a gallery was willing to push it a little bit, contact clients and get them to take a look, and price it reasonably, but not too low. Perceived value means a lot in the works of younger artists.

Would any of these artists grow to be mature and truly talented artists? That was the more difficult question. To try to see what an artist could become.

I worked steadily through the day. Astrid had had food brought to the gallery for lunch, and I can say that in Milan even takeout food is wonderful.

By six I had all the paintings evaluated and grouped into best, good, and fair, and I had little stickers on the back showing suggested pricing.

Several of Astrid's friends had come in during the course of the afternoon to help with moving paintings here and there, hanging paintings and taking them down.

We trooped next door to the Café Averno for a light dinner Astrid had preordered. The food was great, wine was even better, and the people at the table were ebullient—Astrid was beaming. I had clearly met her expectations. But I was exhausted. I finished eating and excused myself, saying I needed to go to my hotel and sleep. The men at our table, there were four of them, rose to their feet—very polite, even the kid with purple hair. Astrid nodded. "You've done a wonderful job today. Thank you so much." She pressed a small bottle of sleeping pills into my hand. "These will help you sleep better." She rolled her eyes heavenward. "I know how tiring it is, airplanes back and forth. You sleep now."

I went outside, turned right, and stopped. The Brera district is full of little boutique craft shops, sidewalk cafés, tiny restaurants, art galleries, and clothing shops on a web of pedestrian-only streets. A wonderful area, but very difficult to navigate. I had no idea where my hotel was.

Astrid came out of the café with one of the young men from our table. "Achille will walk you to your hotel." She pronounced his name "a-shee-lay." He was a nice-looking guy, the only one wearing a sports jacket. He looked a bit older than the rest.

"I am a friend of Astrid's," he said in British-accented English. He steered me to the door of the Hotel Flora, which was literally only a hundred yards from Astrid's gallery, but it was around two corners, and none of the streets were straight. In the bright light at the entrance, I noticed he had the most remarkable gray eyes.

I went upstairs, took a sleeping pill, and slept for fourteen hours.

I stumbled into the gallery the next day at eleven, the two cups of high-octane espresso I'd just drunk clearing the fog out of my mind. I consider myself a hard worker, and when I get started on something, I tend to work steadily until it's done. So today I wanted to review all my evaluations of the paintings, and my rankings, then spend some time arranging them in suggested groupings. Not all paintings show well together, which directly affects their salability. It took all day even with both of Astrid's assistants and several of her friends, including Achille, helping to move paintings here and there, grouping them and regrouping them.

By six we were done. I saw Achille speak briefly to Astrid, then he took my arm and escorted me out into the warm and breezy evening.

"I think you are tired and need fewer people around you this evening. Perhaps you would consider having dinner with me at Ristorante Cansone, across the street from your hotel. The food is good, but not great. But it is quiet."

I gave him my best smile, and we set off for the restaurant.

Over a dinner that was more than good, Achille talked about Astrid and her gallery.

"She has money, so she is not very serious about proper management. It is a hobby for her." He smiled engagingly. "But she is smart and has attracted a good following for her gallery, which helps young artists sell their work. That is what she wants most." He chuckled. "But she is a little"—he tilted his head—"a little disorganized. She was supposed to have all those paintings evaluated a month ago, some selected and on exhibit by now. You saved her. She can say she was waiting for an expert from America, and she can start hanging the new pieces tomorrow."

I nodded.

"I have a suggestion…" He smiled at me and leaned a bit forward. "I hope you won't think me…" He gave an Italianate shrug that could have meant anything. I almost laughed. Living in New York I'd heard all kinds of come-ons and felt confident I could derail anything unappealing without hurting his feelings. "Why not change your ticket," he said earnestly, "and take a two-day vacation before returning to New York? Unless you have…other obligations?" His voice changed a little as he delicately probed to see if I had a boyfriend waiting impatiently for me.

I picked up my glass of wine and studied its dense red color. The waiter mistook that for a request to top off my glass and did so. Achille and I exchanged smiles. I sipped my wine, stalling for time. Achille leaned back a bit. He didn't seem tense the way a lot of guys in New York did when they were propositioning me. I liked his calm self-confidence. I felt like I could say no to him, or I could say yes to him, and either way would be fine.

He was good at being quiet. Most of the people I knew always seemed to feel that silences needed to be filled with talk.

I changed the subject, not because I wanted to ignore Achille's offer, but because a thought had suddenly occurred to me. "Do people here bargain with the gallery owner over the price of a painting?"

He smiled, and I realized once again that I was becoming very attached to that smile. "At the big art galleries downtown, most art is sold by private showings and there is no bargaining," he told me. "But for small galleries like Galerie Etienne, all prices are negotiable. Are you concerned that the prices you put on Astrid's paintings are too high? Too low?"

"I think my pricing is right, but give Astrid a second price, a higher price to allow room for bargaining." He nodded. One of the nicest features of this part of the Brera district is the pedestrian streets—no traffic noise.

"A piece of art has no intrinsic value." I looked into Achille's gray eyes. "Art is only worth what someone thinks it is worth. Pricing is difficult."

"It is the same with stocks and bonds," he said. "Traders like me spend our days guessing what people will be willing to pay for a share in a company. You can put a monetary value on the assets of a company and divide by the number of outstanding shares to get a number, a 'valuation,' but it has little to do with what people are willing to pay for shares in that company."

I thought of my father, hidden behind that gray-stone-walled, electronics-filled building in Geneva drafting the regulatory changes that would move the European currency exchange rates and central bank discount rates. Changing the price of everything in Europe. I wondered if he was happy.

"You are frowning," Achille said.

"Sorry. I was thinking about prices. My father works in Geneva, at Eurovest. The agency that researches and recommends currency valuations, exchange rates, and discount rates."

Achille straightened up in his chair. "I know of Eurovest. A very important agency within the European financial…how do you Americans call it… community? Which seems a strange word. I have a consulting contract with Eurovest. The three Swiss exchanges are to be combined into one, located in Zurich, and they are using the London Exchange as a model. My colleagues and I are developing the transition plan. What is your father's position there? If you don't mind my inquisitiveness."

"Policy director, I think. Will Astrid still be at the gallery? I need to tell her about my pricing before she puts any paintings up."

Achille glanced at his watch. "Seven thirty. She will have gone home. I have her cell phone number, but she seldom answers after hours."

The waiter filled my glass again and I sipped it, savoring its deep flavors. "This is very good."

Achille frowned at his wineglass. "Director of policy. Your father's name is Kavan?"

I nodded.

"Then I am doubly honored to know you. I've met your father several times at the quarterly financial regulatory conclaves Eurovest holds in Geneva." He raised his glass. "To your father."

I sipped. "I'm glad to hear you have a high opinion of my father. I'm sure he is very good at what he does at Eurovest. But he's not so good at other things. He is what we'd call an absentee parent." I shouldn't have said that, but I'd had several glasses of wine.

We sat quietly for a while. "I'll return to my suggestion," Achille said. "There is still snow in the mountains. You ski, don't you?"

I looked him in the eye. "Are you asking me for a date?"

He smiled again. "You New Yorkers are very direct. Yes, I am asking you for a date."

I became conscious of the warm night breeze, the quiet conversations of people at the other tables.

Astrid had privately told me Achille was "good," whatever that might mean. Divorced but not a womanizer. How bad could he be in comparison to

Alex and the other guys I'd dated recently? Those guys were nice enough, but none of them were guys I wanted to spend much time with other than a date every few weeks. But Achille seemed different. He had some depth, and a bit of mystery that I liked.

"Yes," I told him. "I ski." And I knew at that moment I was agreeing to much more than skiing.

"Perhaps we could go to Chamonix. It is not so crowded this late in the season."

I drank the last of my wine and forced myself not to order another one. I liked Achille's company and could have stayed here another hour enjoying the night, but between long hours at Galerie Etienne and residual jetlag, I was exhausted. I should go to the hotel now, work in the gallery tomorrow, then catch the evening flight back to New York.

But I knew I wouldn't do that.

"Let's ski Zermatt," I told him. "But I don't want to leave Milan tomorrow until after I've repriced the paintings for Astrid. And I need to fly back to New York Sunday night at the latest."

He smiled an open smile. "I will make the arrangements. We leave here tomorrow at noon, spend Friday night and Saturday night in Zermatt, then come back to Milano on Sunday in time for you to catch the evening flight to New York."

I pushed back my wine glass. "And now I need to sleep. I'll see you at the gallery at noon tomorrow.

I'll be packed and ready to go." I blew him a kiss and returned to my hotel. I knew we would be spending our nights in the same bed. And that was fine with me. I felt comfortable with Achille even though I'd only known him a few days. He was good-looking, congenial, outgoing in a quiet sort of way, and best of all, able to carry on an unhurried conversation.

It was a great trip. I hadn't told Achille I knew the Sport Hotel Riffelberg at Zermatt where he'd booked us. I'd been there as a kid with my parents the first year we lived in Geneva.

Achille and I seemed made for each other. We spent Friday night together and there was none of the awkwardness or the false posturing I'd experienced with Alex and most of the guys I'd dated in New York. We skied for two hours Saturday morning, then some wine by the hotel fireplace, then lunch, then a nap in our room. In the afternoon we walked a hiking path to a tiny hut that had been converted to a wine bar where we sat on the terrace in the sunshine, the air crystalline and the view immense. At night the moonlit view of the Matterhorn from the window of our room was spectacular. Sunday we skied for a couple of hours, then back to Milan and my flight to New York.

As we said goodbye at the airport, I promised him I'd come back in two months.

Chapter 3

Back in New York I painted every day, sometimes late into the night. And my paintings were good. Not so big as before, not so aggressive, but the compositions held great depth even though my palette remained dark. My selection of color tones was better than ever before.

I found myself smiling a lot. When I wasn't painting I was thinking of Achille. He'd suggested he visit me in New York, but I vetoed that. I needed to keep my concentration. I was fearful he would be offended by that, but he wasn't.

On my next trip I stopped by Astrid's gallery and offered my help, but she just smiled and told me she was fine. Achille had picked me up at the airport, and we drove straight to Basso for dinner. It was a quiet place, less trendy than the restaurants downtown, but the food and wine were the best I have ever had. I had risotto Milanese, of course. Before dinner Achille ordered us each one of those special Negronis made with Campari, red vermouth, and Prosecco instead of gin. I felt great. Achille's smiling face had a lot to do with it. Afterward we strolled a few blocks, window shopping. Milan still has the best clothing styles in Europe, regardless of what the Parisians say.

We had a room at the Hotel Flora, the same hotel I'd stayed at my first visit to Milan. The rooms were surprisingly large.

And Achille was wonderful. We made love, then opened a bottle of Spanish Cava he'd ordered and toasted ourselves.

"It is wonderful to see you, Sarah. I've missed you these two months."

"And I've missed you, Achille." I looked at the lights of the city outside the window sheers. "I hope you understand that I want to see you, as often as I can, but that I have to paint my paintings. I'm just starting my career as a painter and it is important for me to stay concentrated…"

"I understand," he said. And I felt like he really did.

"I probably won't be able to see you more than a week at a time, every couple of months."

"I understand. I also have my work, which is important to me." I knew his stock trading took a lot of time and required him to be available for phone calls any time. "But I plan to work less next year. I may go back to trading on the London Exchange."

"And live in London?"

His expression told me he might, but he said, "No," and I didn't pursue it.

I knew he carried a British passport, had gone to university in Britain, and spoke Italian, German, and British English. But there was an accent, maybe Central European, that crept into his English from time to time. He once mentioned living in Bratislava when he was in elementary school. But he had lived in Milan for the past year. And in Zurich.

I'd always thought it impolite to be too inquisitive about someone's past, and so I assumed Achille would tell me anything that was important for me to know. That is the way I had always felt about someone's past—if it's important they'll tell me, if not, I won't ask. Although I've been known to fabricate parts of my own past and tell it to some guy I'm trying to draw out. I was often surprised by what I heard. Since I never dated any guy for more than a few months, I never worried about being caught out in contradictions.

I didn't fabricate things for Achille though. Instead I talked about the present and the future. From my first visit to Milan, when we'd sat together in the little café around the corner from Galerie Etienne, I'd told him, "I am going to be the best painter I can." Saying this self-affirmation helps me stay focused.

I woke once in the night. Achille is beautiful even sleeping. His expression is calm, his hair perfect.

As I drifted back to sleep I imagined a past for him. A good family living in Bratislava during the communist years, surviving on the tattered remains of a Hapsburg inheritance, living in one of the gray Stalinist apartment blocks. Then one day an uncle smuggles Achille across the border into Austria, they travel to England, he is installed in a boarding school in Surrey, and his life begins. As a precocious eighteen-year-old he enters the London School of Economics, but drops out after a year and a half to work as a day trader for one of the smaller investment houses in the city.

That part I'm pretty sure is true, since one afternoon we had a really fun meet-up with some English guys he knew from his day-trader job in London years ago. Most of the talk was about the consolidation of the Geneva, Bern, and Zurich stock exchanges into a single Swiss Exchange and the opportunities that provided for independent traders. Achille and his friends were careful to include me in the conversation and to make fun of their own mistakes. It was an enjoyable evening even though I got embarrassingly drunk. But so what? Nothing new about that.

Achille seemed to like to live at the edge of the art world, though he was neither an artist nor an art buyer. He did not collect art, but he was very knowledgeable about it and steered influential people toward good purchases. I think he was drawn equally to the people in the art world—the young artists and the small galleries that come and go—as to the art itself.

He once told me he'd returned to university after a year as a trader for Baring's Investments. He seemed to think I would know that name, but I did not and I didn't ask him about it. He completed a degree with second class honors, I think he said it was in classics, at Southampton University. After graduation he went back to stock trading, but this time as an independent.

He'd been divorced for several years when I met him. His ex-wife had custody of their daughter, and that's all I wanted to hear about his former life.

I sensed he missed the stability of marriage, even though I don't believe a marriage certificate will ever provide stability, and I told him so, wondering if I was compromising our relationship; but it is an important point for me. He smiled and called me cynical in a friendly way. He was a very refreshing change from the men I knew in New York.

One evening, after dinner with a lot of wine, he'd said to me, "You have not been married, I think." I told him I had not been married and didn't see myself getting married any time soon. I had too much painting to do; that was my life.

"No one thing should be your life," he told me. "I think for Anna, my ex-wife, having a child was the one thing she wanted from life. But one thing is never enough, not for her, not for anyone." Achille made a gesture I could not interpret.

I stopped myself from telling him I thought his endless phone calls, doing stock trading, appeared to be "that one thing" no one should settle for. But for once I kept my mouth shut.

The next day Achille, clearly embarrassed by his revelations about himself the night before, asked me to go with him to Lugano. "I have always loved Lugano," he told me. "I want you to love it too, and I have a surprise which I am sure you will like."

That statement made me uneasy. I never liked surprises. They too often backfire. I considered telling him I couldn't go with him to Lugano, not this trip, since I really did want to get back to New York. I'd already been away from New York five days on this particular trip and was eager to get back to a painting I had underway.

But...a few more days with Achille...how could I say no?

We left for Lugano that morning. It was a long drive from Milan, but he wanted to drive so that we'd have a car while we were there. It would mean I'd be away from New York almost a week by the time I got back, which violated my own resolution to stay away from painting no longer than five days at a time. I really preferred to paint every day. It was an obsession. But Achille was becoming an obsession too. I was torn. Everything was going well—Astrid's showing of the young artists' work had been a big success. She was effusive in her thanks to me. And Ellis had phoned to tell me that two more of my paintings had sold.

The scenery on the drive to Lake Country was magnificent, but it was thoughts of Achille that occupied my mind as we rolled north in his Alfa Romeo. I liked it here with him, but I knew I would find it difficult, if not impossible, to paint here. If I spent too much time away from the grimy urgency of New York, I'd lose that "intense, secretive" New York persona my father once accused me of having, and of which I was secretly proud. But still, I enjoyed Achille's company more than that of any man I'd ever dated. And I didn't want to lose that either.

"You seem rather full of yourself," I told Achille as we came to the outskirts of Lugano. "This must be quite a surprise."

"Full of myself?" He was concentrating on traffic.

"You seem to have a secret you are very happy with."

He laughed, showing his perfect teeth. "You understand me. And yes, I do have a secret, a gift I hope you will like."

That made me even more nervous. It meant that sometime soon I was going to be shown something and expected to show great surprise and delight. I never liked trying to do a lot of oohing and aahing, even when it was something I liked. But I smiled at him because I could see his smile slipping a little at my lack of enthusiasm.

"I'm sure I will like your surprise," I reassured him.

In Lugano City we drove down the Esplanade along the shore of the lake, blue and placid. On all sides the mountains rose up, snowcapped. Scattered villas were sparks of white among the trees on the mountainsides. It was all exquisitely beautiful. We turned onto Gione Street, which turned into a winding road and began switchbacking its way up the mountainside. Even with daylight almost gone, the view was spectacular.

Achille turned into a driveway through an open gate flanked by two red-and-white pilasters. He parked on the circle driveway in front of a modern house—white with lots of glass.

A man dressed in a white-and-black butler's uniform came out and took our luggage inside. He greeted Achille casually and said a polite hello to me. We followed him in through an entry, then down three steps to the wide living room with an off-white carpet with long pastel swirls in the fabric. There was a long white sofa facing a fireplace sunken two steps below the level of the entry. Above the fireplace the mountains and the lake were a magical vista.

Achille let me absorb the view for a moment. "There is a very nice swimming pool." He indicated the lawn sloping away toward the lake. "Just out of sight. But from the pool you can see the lake." Achille gave me a kiss. "And, of course, the stars above."

The old man in his black-and-white uniform had brought a silver platter with a bottle of champagne and two glasses. "This is Bruno," Achille said. "He has worked for my friends who own this villa for more than thirty years." We toasted each other and the house and the vista.

"It has been a long drive. Let's take a swim," he said.

"There are robes and some new swimming suits in our room. Let's change and drink champagne in the pool."

Outside the air was cold; the warm pool water steamed mistily into the night. The champagne was crisp, and overhead I could see stars in the clear mountain air.

"This is lovely," I told Achille. "You said friends of yours owned this villa. Are they here now?"

He shook his head. "No, Arturo and Sylvie, who own Villa Fiore, are at their townhouse in London. We have the place to ourselves."

That first night at Villa Fiore was as magical as honeymoons are supposed to be.

The next morning my mind raced, trying to absorb all the beauty I was surrounded with. Eventually I was able to clear my mind and simply sit in the sunshine on the terrace, daydreaming the way I had as a child. Achille was in the little office making more of his endless phone calls. Bruno brought coffee and croissants.

We stayed at Villa Fiore for two perfect days and nights.

One evening as the sun slid behind the mountains, we drove down to the Esplanade and had dinner at one of the restaurants along the lakefront. Then Achille took me to a place a little farther down the Esplanade where there was a very nice little orchestra playing American 1940s music, with a slow enough tempo that we could dance. I remembered enough of my dance lessons to be able to foxtrot and waltz. Then the drive up the mountain to our Shangri-la.

How could I not have fallen in love? I flew back to New York glowing.

Chapter 4

In New York I worked at my painting with a clarity I'd never felt before. The paintings composed themselves under my brush, one after the next. My canvases got large again, but the figures in them were better composed, not so raw, flesh tones more luminous, and overall a greater fluency of brushwork.

And, I knew that in two months I'd fly to Milan and Achille would be waiting. We'd drive to Lugano and up the winding road to beautiful Villa Fiore, which felt like returning to paradise.

The days would pass like a dream. Then an evening would come, usually while Achille and I were sitting by the fireplace with a cognac at hand, when I would say, "Much as I love you and this Shangri-la, I need to go back to New York. I need to paint."

He would always say, "I understand." And I loved him best for that understanding.

We loved the cafés and restaurants and clubs of the Brera district in Milan, but we loved Lugano and the wonderful Villa Fiore more.

Achille told me that if Arturo was using the villa, he could book us a room at the old Hotel Splendide: a great stone pile on the lakeshore, one of the oldest hotels in Lugano, but beautifully refitted inside.

When I returned to New York, my apartment felt like a dark and dirty closet. But I found myself doing some of my most inspired work. My paintings were still what some called "dark," but now they were subtly different, more mature. I could tell they were good, very good. I felt I was expressing some of the mysteries of the human heart. Ellis took them all and told me my sales were steady. "You've developed a following."

I laughed, but I was secretly very proud of that accomplishment. We were sitting in Tempus Gallery, at the little desk, when he told me. He handed me a check for an amount that surprised me, then rushed off to deal with a client. Walking back to my apartment, I felt that same tingle, that same irrepressible urge to laugh out loud, just for the sheer joy of being alive.

"I'm in love," I said out loud. "And I can paint!" Passersby ignored me. This is New York.

The downstairs door buzzer was blasting. I glanced at the clock from my nest of blankets: ten a.m. Who'd be up at this hour?

I got up and pressed the speaker button. "Who is it?"

"Lisa."

"Lisa?"

"Your sister, dammit. Open up! It's freezing down here."

I hit the release and pulled a sweater over the other layers I had on. I looked a mess, having slept in my clothes again after working on a painting until three that morning.

I opened the door and someone I didn't recognize stepped in. Lisa, elegant, mysterious, bold, all sharp edges and dramatic flair. She walked in like she owned the place and started examining the painting on my easel. "Caravaggio-like, this one. Moody. Are you moody these days, Sarah?" She toured the rumpled apartment, the bedroom jammed with paint supplies, the tiny bathroom, and what laughably passed for a kitchen. "Got anything to drink?"

I poured out two generous shots of Bushmills and handed her one. Her nails were perfect in violet enamel, not excessively long, but elegant. In fact, she was elegant in all respects except her attitude. Her walk, her clothing, her accent, all very European. Her language was now seasoned with bits of British English and French. And she was not shy about slipping in occasional whole phrases in French. Intended to impress the dull monolingual American—me.

We circled my cluttered apartment like tigers in a cage.

"I'm realizing how powerful Father's position is," Lisa said. "The power of knowledge…knowledge of the future, of knowing where prices are going, knowing it before anyone else."

"You sound like you're spending a lot of time with him. More time than he ever gave me."

She drank half her drink. "Yeah, guess I'm the lucky one."

"What the hell is that supposed to mean?"

"Mother abandoned me to go off with you to Florida…"

"To help Grandfather's dying!" I snapped. "And anyway, you said you wanted to stay with Father."

Lisa's tone was smug. "No matter. That's past. I talk to Mother on the phone occasionally. And I talk to Father every month or so when he drives over to Davos. Not that I do much talking. The stresses inside Eurovest are intense, so he does all the talking. Venting, you Americans would call it. He told me recently that when I graduate and go into finance, never trust anyone." A strange expression came over Lisa's face. "Ironic, I guess, that he trusts me."

"What's that supposed to mean?"

Lisa shrugged and sipped from her drink.

"Why are you here?" I asked. "Not that I'm not glad to see you, but I thought we'd decided to go skiing together…sometime." I'd forgotten what I'd agreed to.

"Yeah. So when will you be in Chamonix?"

"I can't say right now," I told her. "I've got to stay at my painting, get my name known. Selling art is competitive."

"But you take time off to go see your boyfriend in Milano."

"You know, Lisa, your sniping tone is offensive." I poured myself another stiff drink and tossed it down. "Let's quit this bickering, OK?"

Lisa sat down, crossed her legs, and began swinging one foot in a way she knew would irritate me.

"By the way, Achille seems nice. I met him at Galerie Etienne." Her tone made me uneasy. *Would Lisa make moves on Achille?*

I looked at the grimy window.

"I'm thinking about moving to Florida," Lisa said.

"That's ridiculous. With just a few months left until you graduate, plus all this knowledge and power from Father." I spread my arms to indicate its vastness. "And the connections you'll have being a Rossey alumna… you're going to quit and hide in Florida?"

"You did. And besides, I think Mother could use my help. I don't think she's well."

"What the hell are you talking about?"

"Forget it." She snorted a bitter laugh. "I'll graduate and go into finance and who knows, maybe one day I'll even be considered as good as Father is."

I wanted to tell her she sounded like some junior high school girl pouting because people paid attention to her father and not her.

"Maybe I'll even be as successful as you," she snapped.

I waved at the apartment. "You won't have to work very hard to do better than this."

She glared at the grunge on the window glass. "You've got people you can trust. That's important. Can I trust you?" Her tone had changed to something like pleading.

"How do you expect me to answer that?" I said. I put my glass to my lips even though I really didn't want whiskey right now.

I was horrified to see a tear run down Lisa's cheek. This hip, tough young woman who had come through my door thirty minutes ago was now my pathetic little sister, crying into her glass.

After a minute's snuffling she said, "You want to know something? I always envied you. Because you were Father's favorite, and you still are."

I scrambled for a response. "You're the one he comes to visit, not me."

"And you have Achille," Lisa muttered.

I nodded.

"And you're a successful painter," Lisa kept on.

I nodded.

"You have it all," Lisa muttered to the floor. "But I'm beginning to make my own success. You'll see."

"Exactly what will I see?"

"A new me." Lisa smiled a brittle smile and became the hip young thing she'd been thirty minutes ago. "Come to Chamonix. We'll go skiing. I'll buy your ticket."

She stepped into the bathroom and adjusted her makeup.

"Skiing," I said. "Remember when we were kids, Christmas at Zermatt, learning to ski?" I asked her.

"No. I learned to ski at Courchevel, the Rossey school has a…"

"You don't remember Christmas at Zermatt; I was ten, you were six? The first year we were in Geneva."

"No." Lisa shrugged. "Anyway. Come to Switzerland. We'll go skiing."

I nodded. "I will, but I've got to get this work done first." I waved at the painting on the easel. "My stuff is selling, and I don't want to…"

"You can spare a few days…"

"Not right away," I hedged. "I've got several more canvases to finish up. My show is already scheduled, and I can't let Ellis give my turn to someone else. The art scene is not very forgiving…."

Lisa finished her drink and started pacing. "I don't think you know much about unforgiving situations." She shrugged again as though the whole conversation was becoming tedious. "Well then, without taking too much time away from your unforgiving schedule, show me a little of New York. Just today. I'm flying back tomorrow morning."

"Tomorrow morning?" I put my glass of whiskey aside. "You flew over here for one day?"

"Three days. One day to see you, and two days visiting Mother. Yesterday and the day before."

That surprised me. "Visiting Mother?"

"St. Pete is really a boring town. But I owed Mother a visit. She came to see me last year, we were planning to do some sightseeing in the Alps, but she didn't feel well. I think it was the altitude. We went down to Milan for a few days instead."

"Did you go to Geneva?"

"With Mother? Of course not."

After a while we put our coats on and ventured out into grimy old New York. We visited Tempus Gallery and Astrid's 404 Gallery, and MOMA, which bored Lisa, and then stopped by the studio of an artist friend of mine. We had dinner together, and afterward I dragged myself to a nightclub I used to go to. But none of it was any fun. Lisa was arrogant, competing with me for the attention of everyone we talked to.

The next morning, hung over as usual, I smiled and waved as her taxi departed for the airport. I was glad she was gone—she wore me out. And despite her almost constant talk, I sensed she never really got around to some topic she wanted to talk about, like she couldn't quite bring herself to do so.

I started painting but found my attention wandering. Instead I took up my usual seat on the window ledge. What had happened to the little sister I remembered so fondly, with her shy smile and quiet voice? What had she become? What had I become? I started crying. She didn't even remember that Christmas in Zermatt.

My sister and I played games in our room using a couple of worn dolls we'd brought, creating stories and landscapes. Mother and Father read and sometimes read to us. On Christmas morning our parents gave Lisa and me two books each. One of mine, I remember, was about dinosaurs. Lisa and I read our books, played with dolls, or sometimes just sat and daydreamed while the sun glittered on the snowfields outside and the skiers gracefully slalomed down the slopes. The time passed dreamlike.

For Christmas Eve dinner we dressed up. Father had on a suit, Mother wore a green dress and her pearls, Lisa and I each had on a new dress we'd just bought down in Zermatt village. In the dining room the scent of the fresh-cut Christmas tree was sharp and sweet. It was decorated with real candles, which made my father and mother exchange nervous looks. A chorus of kids from the village sang after dinner.

Christmas day Father had arranged for Lisa and me to take ski lessons. I learned quickly on the short beginner's skis they rented us, but little Lisa kept falling down. After an hour she told Mother she was cold and wanted to quit. I remember giving Lisa a covert look of superiority. And I could tell by her expression I had hurt her. I have regretted my hurtful glance all the years since then.

That vacation was the last time our whole family was together and happy.

And Lisa said she remembered none of it. I had planned to apologize to her for that hurtful glance I gave her. But if she doesn't remember it, I can certainly forget it.

I resolved that before this ski season ended I would take a few days, fly to Switzerland, and go skiing with Lisa. And late this year I would fly down to St. Pete and spend a few days with Mother.

I slept for a while then went back to work on a half-finished canvas. But after a few minutes I set it aside and began painting a portrait in vermillion and indigo, a portrait of Lisa. It flowed quickly onto the canvas. I mixed colors that were delicate and subtle for the shadowing. As if by magic the tonality was in perfect accord with her expression. I captured her stylishness, her pride, her intelligence, and a bit of contempt. She was glancing down and to the side, her mind on something. She was not happy, not unhappy. I finished it in four hours, slept for a while, ate something, and went back to the other canvases I owed Ellis. For a week I did nothing but eat, sleep, and paint. Then I collapsed for a while, sleeping and daydreaming—my usual post-painting stupor. I called Ellis and he came up and I showed him my eight new pieces but not the vermillion and indigo portrait of my sister. I hid that one away. He spent a few minutes looking at the other paintings and emoting his usual deep cogitation. "I'll take all of them."

He extracted a check from his jacket pocket and handed it to me. "Here's a check for your last two sales. I'll send Frederick up to get these paintings this afternoon."

I looked at the check. "Should be good for a few days in Italy."

Ellis shook his head and buttoned his overcoat. "Easy come, easy go," he intoned with an air of deep profundity. He likes to take on the persona of an academic, pursing his lips, peering over the tops of his glasses. But I've seen his résumé: a business degree from City College of New York.

After Ellis was gone I contacted Achille. "Villa Fiore?"

"Yes."

"And you won't spend all your time on the phone this time?"

He laughed. "I promise."

Chapter 5

Achille and I had eaten a late dinner at Il Ottavi—a quiet lakeside restaurant we liked—then back to Villa Fiore and straight to bed. We'd made love with the drapes open and the pool lights off. I remember stars above the mountains being bright in the sky as I dozed off.

Bruno whispering to Achille at the bedroom door wakened me. I caught the words *telefono* and *Signorina Sarah*. Bruno looked tousled.

The clock beside the bed said 02:00.

Achille, in his dark blue robe, came back and stood beside the bed. He reached under the covers and very gently took my hand. I felt dread rising up in my mind. "You are awake?"

"Yes."

"There is a phone call for you. Your father."

"Calling me at this hour?"

"Yes."

I scrambled out of bed, tossed on a robe, and went out to the kitchen. Arturo and Sylvie thought of a phone as something for servants, so there was only one in the whole house, and it was in the kitchen.

I picked up the antique white receiver. "Hello?"

"It's your father, Sarah. I'm sorry to disturb you, but there is…I have some rather bad news, I'm afraid." My heart began to race.

"Your sister Lisa has been in a car crash. Route 16 just up the mountain from Lugano. Her car ran off the road…" His voice caught. "I'm afraid she is dead."

I couldn't breathe, tears flooded my eyes, then the air came out of my lungs in something like a cough. I managed to ask, "When?"

"Tonight, a few hours ago. Achille is there?"

"Yes."

"Stay with him. The company plane will bring me to Lugano tonight. I will talk with the police. There is nothing you can do. I'll phone you in the morning."

"And Mother?"

"I phoned her and told her it was pointless for her to come all the way to Switzerland. There is nothing to be done here except final arrangements, which I will make."

He hung up, and Achille stepped forward.

"My sister is dead. A car crash," I choked.

He held me in a close embrace while I sobbed for a time. Then he half-carried me to the couch in front of the fireplace. Bruno had brought the whiskey bottle and glasses. I downed a double, then a second one, but it had no effect.

Lisa is gone. Gone forever.

"Don't drink more," Achille said, taking the empty glass out of my hand. "Take a sleeping medicine, then sleep. Don't think about this. Not now, not tonight."

The whiskey and the pills did their job. I was soon in bed and unconscious. When I woke it was a bright morning, the mist still on the surface of the lake. I felt miserable.

Achille drove me to the police office where he helped my father complete the forms having to do with a foreigner dying in Switzerland. It was apparently very complicated. Police came and went; forms were filled out; coffee was brought. The police were cordial, but it seemed endless. Sometimes I would go outside and walk up and down the block, then back to wait on the wooden bench.

Eventually Achille and my father emerged from the back office.

"I think perhaps it is better if you go with your father to Geneva," Achille said. He shook hands with my father. I heard my father thank him and apologize for something. Then a taxi took my father and me to the airport. He stared out the window while I stared out the other window the whole trip. Neither of us spoke.

I felt like I should comfort my father, or maybe he should comfort me. But neither of us said anything.

On the flight to Geneva my father gave me a copy of the police report. Lisa's Mercedes had skidded on icy Route 16 coming down the mountain toward Lugano town. A winter driving accident, nothing more.

Nothing more...

Of Lisa's life there would never be anything more.

It was mid-afternoon by the time we landed, and it took another fifteen minutes to get out of the Executive Air terminal. A Eurovest car drove us to the apartment.

"I've arranged for Lisa's body to be cremated," my father told me. "I don't want a service of any kind. We—you, your mother, and I—will speak of this later when...time has passed. You are welcome to stay here, but I am going to be working, so if you would rather return to New York, that might be best."

I nodded, still not able to think clearly. I was relieved there would be no service for Lisa—that would have been too painful. There were no available flights back to New York that night, so I spent an hour at evening time walking the lakeshore in a cold wind, then spent the night in the guest bedroom and caught a taxi to the airport the next morning.

My father had already left for his office.

My apartment, cluttered with paints and easels and canvases, felt like a cave. It held no comfort for me. I resolved to move, but did nothing about it. For the rest of that day I sat in the one chair, jet-lagged, drinking

Bushmills out of a semi-clean cup until the bottle was empty and I dozed off.

Next day I pulled myself together, unpacked, cleaned myself up, and went to Tempus Gallery.

"Good news," the girl told me. "Two more of your works have sold."

I shrugged, looked briefly at the art currently on display, and went back to the apartment and resumed painting. My response to tragedy.

But the painting I was working on stalled. I set it aside, got a clean canvas, and started another one that had been in my head a long time, an abstraction of three people in the middle distance in Battery Park on a rainy day. And even though that image had been in my mind for several months, and I knew it had potential, I could not seem to get started right. The harder I tried the worse things got. I painted over the canvas and left it on the easel. Achille phoned and we talked, but it was a strained and meaningless conversation—my fault—I just didn't want to talk, about Lisa or about anything. My father phoned, and that conversation was no better.

I wandered New York City, not bothering with the art museums or galleries that were my usual refuges. I just wandered the streets. Then to the Thorn and Thistle for happy hour, then home.

Achille called again.

"We need to talk in person," he said. "Come to Milan."

My apartment had become like a prison, my painting was stalled, and I was tired of wandering the streets even though the weather had been quite nice lately. "I'll fly to Milan tomorrow, then let's go to Lugano," I told him. "But not to Villa Fiore. Book a room at the Splendide."

A day and a half later I was in Milan. I had to take a connecting flight through London, so didn't get into Milan until evening. Achille was waiting. We started for Lugano in his Alfa.

In the car, I dozed off as night fell. And I found myself in a nightmare, driving fast, too fast, down the mountain switchbacks toward the lights of Lugano. Rain is turning to snow, but I speed on. I need to meet someone; it is urgent. The tires slip as I enter the next set of turns, and I press the accelerator pedal down a touch to regain traction. All my senses are sharp and focused, but as I let my foot off the accelerator I know it is too late. I am going too fast for the next turn. The car smashes through the guardrail and out into darkness. In that final instant, I sense the presence of a familiar person. I expect them to save me somehow. I start to call out, but then the car impacts frozen rock, and my time is gone.

I started awake and fumbled in my purse for a cigarette.

"Don't smoke in the car," Achille said. He down-shifted and gave me a look. "Nightmare?"

I powered the window down and tossed the cigarette into the night rain that had turned to snow. "No," I lied smoothly. "No, just tension over…Lisa's death. I let her slip away. I let her die."

"No one 'lets' someone die," he said softly.

"She visited me in New York last February. I think she wanted to discuss something with me, but I'm not sure. I think she wanted something, but I don't know what. I should have tried harder to…"

"To what?" Achille said. There was an edge of irritation in his voice that I was not used to.

Traffic was a long, blurred curve of red taillights that evolved into individual pairs as we approached the Swiss border. We inched along, showed our passports at the checkpoint, and then continued down the mountain toward Lugano. A veil of snow covered the lights of the city below.

As Achille carefully navigated the last switchback, I slumped in the pale leather seat and wished for a cigarette.

"Try to relax," Achille said, softening his tone with a smile that seemed forced. Maybe Lisa's death and our back-and-forth relationship had worn down that Milano charm that used to thrill me so. I felt guilty about not spending more time with him, but my painting was important to me. I felt guilty about being so sorrowful now, but Lisa's death had shocked me. I knew I was not good company, but I was not able to force myself to be cheerful. Maybe my long-distance relationship with Achille just could not succeed.

At the hotel Achille spent some time on the phone, apparently with less-than-positive results. He hung up the phone, glared at it for a moment, then wrapped himself in one of the plush blankets and took a bottle of Glenfiddich out to the terrace and sat in the cold night wind. I stripped off my clothes and slid into bed.

I dreamt I was back on the mountain road. It's pitch-black night, and I've been in a car accident. I'm lying on the wet asphalt with flashing ambulance lights all around. I know that someone else will make all the decisions now, and the thought is somehow comforting.

I smell wet pavement and warm antifreeze from the smashed radiator. Lisa leans over me, and then suddenly I'm looking down at Lisa lying on the wet asphalt. She looks very peaceful, dressed in those flashy boutique throwaway clothes she could always make look great. She's dying. I touch her hand. It's already going cold.

When I woke, the morning light filtering through a layer of clouds made the lake and the mountains shades of gray and silver. Achille was asleep beside me. I ordered room service—coffee, croissants, and some newspapers—then sat before the window wrapped in a hotel robe, watching the wind gust great fans on the surface of the lake.

Achille slept through my rustling around. He could sleep anywhere, through any kind of racket. Me, I had trouble sleeping even in my own bed. A good night's sleep was precious. I was well aware that coffee, cigarettes, sleeping pills, whiskey, and Valium didn't help.

The Hotel Splendide faces the lake, getting the full force of the springtime winds coming down the valley. The tall windows rattled, and there was a hint of a draft. From time to time, rain walked across the pewter surface of the lake. I found my eye analyzing the shades of gray as I leafed through the arts sections of the *Milano Espress*, then the *Geneva Times*. The television was on with no sound; *Plein Soleil* was playing. Alain Delon had wrapped his murdered friend's body in the shroud while the wind whipped the sails of the sloop Marge, driving it toward the empty Mediterranean horizon. My self-pity leaked back in around the edges, along with an irrational resentment of Achille.

After he woke, our conversation deteriorated into bickering. I paced, he paced. After a while I packed my suitcase. Achille sat in the white chair by the window, drinking coffee and leafing moodily through the business section of *München Zeitgeist*.

I took my coat and suitcase to the door. "I can't be with you right now, Achille."

He said nothing.

"I need to be alone...for a while." I stood there, my hand on the door lever, wondering what I was waiting for. More definitive pronouncements seemed too difficult, so I opened the door and left.

The hotel car took me to the Ringenplatz in downtown Lugano, and from the row of business hotels I picked the Alpine Hotel at random. In my room, I turned on the TV and watched the end of *Plein Soleil*, hating it as always because it feels like the director and the screenwriter just ran out of time, energy, and ideas. I felt the same about myself.

When I woke up, I was lying on the bed in my clothes. There was a Mexican soap opera on Star TV from Munich dubbed in German. I called room service and worked my way through a bottle of Rozzoli Cabernet, then another one while the day came and went. I alternately prodded myself to get up and do something and laid comatose, staring at the television. It all seemed like too much trouble, so I continued to lie there in the gray flicker, anxious and restless and too tired to move. Eventually, I fell asleep again.

When I woke a dismal rain was clicking on the window. The clock said 07:00. I took a shower, went downstairs, and drank an espresso at the stand-up hotel coffee bar. Then I bought an umbrella in the gift shop and walked four blocks to the Viaggio Art Museum. My usual response to stress is to seek out good art and immerse myself in it. It hadn't been working in New York, but now I felt like it would. I walked past the modern stuff and into the hall where I knew they had a Caravaggio on permanent display along with some of the Dutch masters. The Caravaggio somehow soothed me a bit. Made me want to resume my painting. I moved on to some of the Dutch paintings and was standing in front of Rembrandt's *Young Girl Leaning on a Windowsill,* on loan from a museum in London. The composition and the girl's expression were wonderful. I was enthralled. There was a touch on my shoulder. It was my father.

It was disorienting to see him here, dressed in a conservative Bottega suit accented by a gray silk tie. He is not a tall man, but solid and muscular, not much aged from his book jacket photos, an echo of Karsh's photo of Hemingway—perfect silver hair, gray eyes.

He smiled uncertainly. "Dutch masters? You've changed."

He took my arm and steered me into the museum tea shop full of espresso steam and the waitstaff's chatter in Italian and German. We both ordered hot chocolate and sat looking at the rain falling on the hedges outside.

"Letting your hair grow out," he said finally.

"Why are you here?" I asked. "Sorry. I don't mean to be so abrupt."

"I wanted to see you. I'm on my way to the States. Achille called me; he said he was worried about you."

My irritation surged. "He should not take it on himself to report my condition to you."

My father touched my arm. "Lisa's death has hurt all of us. Achille told me you had decided not to see him for a while. I...feel saddened by that, Sarah." He rubbed the blonde wood veneer of the tabletop.

I stiffened. "I just need to be by myself for a while."

"Well…" My father stared at the tabletop. "I worry you are by yourself too much, Sarah." He paused, searching for words. "Aside from my concern for you, there is something else we need to discuss."

I stood up, trembling with anger. "No," I said. "Not right now. I don't want to talk about me or Lisa or Achille, or anything else!"

"Sit down, Sarah," he said. "I think there are things you need to know…"

Suddenly I could stand it no longer. "I can't hear about these things right now!"

I ran out of the tea shop and rushed down the street in the rain.

Chapter 6

In New York I went straight to my easel, set up a canvas. I had in mind an abstract that I had been thinking about for a long time, but the fall of the light on the forms in the centerline of the painting had not been clear before. Now it felt like it was. I mixed colors and started painting.

It went together with amazing speed. I started another painting and then another. I expected my father to call, but he did not. I told myself that was what I wanted. I painted ferociously, huge scarlet and umber paintings, human figures in a twilight world, beset by immense forces, their line and form fluid.

Every day, I ate whatever the daily special was at the Thorn and Thistle—the pub down the street—drank Bushmills whiskey, and painted. I began buying pre-stretched canvases so big I could barely get them up the stairs and into the door of my apartment.

New York City is an ideal place to isolate yourself from the world. Sometimes someone would buzz the door release, but I would ignore it.

I left the sofa bed pulled out and the dirty sheets and blankets on it, so that when exhaustion of mind and the fog of alcohol overtook me, day or night, I would lie down on the bed, wrap the tangle of blankets around me, and sleep until the fire in my brain woke me and drove me back to the easel.

The only people I saw for months were the barman at the Thorn and Thistle and Ellis—every month I would haul five or six big canvases down the street to Tempus Gallery.

"You look like hell, Sarah," Ellis said, setting my twine-tied canvases against the gallery wall outside the door of his office. "What are you doing to yourself?"

"Got a cigarette?" I asked, sitting on the metal chair opposite his desk.

"No, I don't. And there's no smoking in the gallery. You need a decent meal, not a cigarette."

I ignored him. After a moment we stepped over to my paintings, I untied the twine, and he flipped through them. "Leave the paper between them for a while," I told him. "The paint's barely dry."

"Jesus," he muttered. "From what labyrinth of your mind are you dredging up these images?"

"Could you hang them as a group?" I asked. "Maybe over there, on the left wall as people walk in." I pointed at a row of undistinguished still lifes on the left wall.

"Did your assistant, what's her name, suggest this arrangement?"

"She quit. I laid that out myself."

"It's not right," I told him. "But if you took it down, put up six or seven of my canvases along here, that would bring people in. You could move these still lifes back there where the light is less white."

"I'll think about it," he said breathing out his I-get-so-sick-of-artists-telling-me-how-to-run-my-gallery sigh. "And by the way, would you like to work here part time? I need some help." He walked me to the door. It was overcast with a cold wind blowing down Essex Street.

"I'll think about it," I told him, echoing his tone.

"You go to Beekman's, get a decent meal, then go home and get some sleep, and quit drinking so much," he told me. "I'll let you know about these paintings in a day or two. If you go to work for me you can start arranging your own artwork."

I left but didn't go to Beekman's restaurant. Instead I went to the Thorn and Thistle, sat at the bar and ate whatever slop they were serving for lunch, bought a bottle of Bushmills (the barman sold it to me under the counter at cost), and went home.

The next day I walked by the front window of Tempus Gallery, and Ellis had four of my big black-and-red canvases hanging in a row on the left wall of the gallery, near the front, just as I'd suggested. He'd turned more of the ceiling track lights onto them, and they burned under the harsh white light. I stood outside, leaning against the wall beside the gallery windows, watching people passing. Without exception their eyes turned to the paintings as they hurried past. Several paused for a few seconds.

I went inside and found Ellis in his jumbled office. "What are the hours for this part-time work you mentioned?"

"Noon to six three days per week."

"When can I start?"

"Tomorrow."

The months went by; I painted and worked at the gallery—that's all. My mother phoned once, and I tried to be upbeat and interested in her doings, but the conversation fell flat. We just couldn't seem to connect about anything except on the most superficial level. I think she wanted me to come to Florida for a visit, but I maneuvered the conversation so she never got to ask. Right now I really didn't want to spend time with my mother. Later, yes, but not now.

My paintings changed. They became smaller and less dark, fewer people, lots of somewhat cubist forms along with letters from an unknown alphabet. I rather liked them, but when I showed several of them to Ellis, he was unimpressed.

"People like your work as it is, Sarah; don't change." He pointed to my big black-and-red stuff.

I didn't bother trying to explain to him that I had little control over the images that floated out of my imagination and onto canvas. I controlled the brush, and my techniques were getting pretty good, I knew that. And I had a good eye for composition. But the source of the imagery was not within my control.

The crusted black ice in the gutters was melting as spring came to New York. One morning the sound of rain woke me at four. I took my coffee to my usual early morning seat in the window frame overlooking the dark street.

As the gray light behind the clouds brightened, I realized I'd been thinking about how the surface of Lake Lugano had that same burnished pewter color in winter. I hadn't been back to Europe since the day I walked out on Achille.

I painted for a couple of hours, finishing up a small canvas in a palette mostly gold and black and chartreuse.

The downstairs door buzzed. I let whoever it was in, and when I unchained the apartment door, Achille was standing there with a box of flowers and two bottles of wine. One was a Veuve Clicquot.

"Hello, Sarah. Is it too early?"

"Achille! Come in," I said, scrambling to reorient myself. He looked exactly the same as when I'd seen him last—dark hair cut short, sports jacket, no tie, a calm demeanor and an easy smile.

He opened the champagne, found a couple of coffee cups that weren't too dirty, poured, and handed me one. The box contained a dozen lavender roses.

"Very beautiful," I said. There was nothing to put them in, so I settled for moving my paint box to the floor and spreading the roses across the scarred oak table top. "What are we celebrating?"

He smiled. That hadn't changed—that open, easy, Milano charm smile. "Maybe I celebrate seeing you again?"

We toasted each other. The wine was sharp and cold, and soon it started to work its way past last night's sleeping pills. Achille prowled around, studying my finished and half-finished work. "Your work is changing."

"Those are the newest ones over there."

He looked carefully at each of my recent paintings in turn.

"Sold two last month. But they don't sell as fast as my work used to. But Tempus Gallery is still carrying my work," I told him. "I'm working there now, part time."

He sat down in the chair, and I sat on the window ledge not saying anything. I had forgotten Achille's pleasing ability to know when to be quiet.

"I'm glad you stopped by," I said, realizing it was true. "I should have told you long ago that I was sorry. Sorry I walked out on you with no explanation. It's just…I'm sorry. Maybe we can consider this champagne a reconciliation gift, except I should have bought it for you."

He smiled.

"That day in Lugano, when I left," I continued, "I wasn't going anywhere. I just needed time by myself. I felt guilty about my sister's death, guilty for not being the big sister she deserved, or the daughter my mother deserved. Or the daughter my father deserves." I ran out of breath. "Sorry. I explain too much." I poured us both another cup of champagne. "I assume you are still living in Milan…"

"No. London. I visit Milano occasionally, and Lugano too, but not so often."

I didn't really want to hear too much about his life—there would certainly be women in it—so I quickly said, "I'm working part time at Tempus."

"You mentioned that already. I think you will do well there; you are very organized, Sarah, as well as being a great artist. My daughter has an interest in art."

And I definitely didn't want to hear about his former wife and kid, so I hurriedly said, "Well, you should caution her not to make art her whole life."

He laughed a gentle laugh and looked theatrically around my apartment entirely given over to painting.

I smiled. "OK, maybe tell her art shouldn't be more than 90 percent of her life anyway. You once told me something about 'no one thing' should be our lives."

"I remember," he said. "Maybe that is true, maybe not." We finished off the champagne. "I'd like for you to come with me for a few minutes," Achille said. "If you have time. Right now. And perhaps you could wear that purple toque if you still have it. I always liked the way it looked on you." His way of saying my hair was a mess. "Open the other bottle of wine and bring it along," he added.

We took a taxi up Lexington Avenue in a light rain. Achille had the driver stop in front of the Metropolitan Museum of Art.

"So…why are we here?" I asked.

"Look there."

At the sidewalk café across the street from the Met entrance, a few people were seated at the outside tables under the awning, despite the rain. A man had his hand raised. It was my father.

"Nice seeing you again, Sarah," Achille said. "I have to go now, but this is also what we are celebrating."

I stepped out, the wine bottle under my arm, and the car pulled away.

I joined my father at the table. "What is this, a conspiracy?" I asked.

"Coffee?" he asked, eyeing the wine bottle. "No, I guess not." The waiter appeared with two wine glasses and poured us each one.

"Before you say anything," my father said, "let me say this: Lisa died in a car accident, and that accident had nothing to do with you. She told the Rossey School she was going to Courchevel, but drove to

Lugano instead." He hesitated. The propane heater was keeping the table a little too warm. My father studied his hands, rubbing the tablecloth. "It's time to stop blaming yourself for not being the sister you think Lisa wanted. I discussed this at length with Mlle Rozier, who was very proud of Lisa's academic achievement at Rossey. She called her brilliant, highly motivated, but prone to…taking chances. And her friend Aurora Tessier turned out not to be the friend Lisa thought she was." He grimaced. "And for that matter, I wasn't the right influence on her either. I should not have been telling confidential matters to anyone, least of all an aggressively competitive nineteen-year-old girl."

"Think I'm like she was? Untrusting, competitive, a chance-taker?" I said.

"Hard-working, yes, untrusting and an extreme chance-taker, no," he said, but his tone was not convincing. "You're different, Sarah. I wouldn't call you untrusting—you trust people, but you can trust them because you don't need them. You don't seem to need anybody in your life. Your art is enough. I know that is not true, but that is an impression you give, sometimes. I recommend you try to change that."

"Achille?" I said, refilling my wine glass.

He looked away. "That is for you, and him, to decide."

I held on to my smile. "You don't need to worry about me. I don't plan to get back together with Achille, despite all his good qualities. And I fully understand that there's more to life than art or the stock market. I'm just working hard, trying to make my mark, like you did."

His steady gray eyes searched mine. "Perhaps it's time to move past that search for recognition and start working on satisfaction instead. I'm very proud of your art, by the way. And I try not to inquire about your personal relationships."

"Thank you. My art is fine. My personal relationships are OK. Achille and I are just friends now."

"Friendship is a very good thing, Sarah," he said. "And in your professional life, I believe you will have many more successes. Whether it's painting or gallery management."

I put down my wine glass and poured myself some coffee.

"All right. Let's toast the future, whatever it brings." We touched glasses, and he went back to staring at the cars sheening past in the rain. After a while, he rose from the café chair reluctantly.

"I have to leave…for the airport. It was my idea to ask Achille to contact you and bring you here. I hope you are not offended."

"I'm not. It is good to see you and good to see Achille."

After his taxi pulled away, I sat watching the cars flashing past in the rain for a while longer.

Many more successes.

My paintings were still good, I knew that. Good enough to sell steadily, but maybe not as good as they used to be. That obsessive fever I used to feel was fading. *Maybe I'll feel it again sometime, maybe not. Maybe it's gone forever.*

April's breezes had finally come to Manhattan. Tempus Gallery was closed Mondays, but I was in the gallery, doing some paperwork. I'd left the front doors open, and people would drift in from time to time, which was OK with me.

I was sitting with my feet up on the desk in the tiny office in the back when I heard footsteps on the hardwood floor. I had gotten so I could tell by the sound of people's steps whether they were likely to buy or not, and these were not the steps of a buyer. They weren't hesitant, but they weren't purposeful either, and there was a strange familiarity about their cadence. I got up and went out to see who was there.

My father was standing in front of a big bold piece done in dark red with a lot of abstract expressionist overtones.

"Hello, Sarah," he said. "Just came in to say hello. I called Ellis yesterday, and he said you would be in today."

"I'm here and I'm doing fine." I waved at the art on the walls. "This is some good work," I said, pointing at a subtle gray-and-purple piece I liked. "But hard to hang. They don't fit together in a way that has any flow to it." I turned back to him. "If I hadn't been here this afternoon, would you have called me at home? It's OK to talk on the phone, you know. Some people even enjoy it."

"I wanted to see you in person, see how you look, get you to stop smoking."

We sat down in the chairs at the little table by the front door.

"I like it here," I told him. "Ellis doesn't want to be tied to the gallery every day, and he trusts me. He can see that I'm the kind of organized person who can do this, so he's given me free rein. Tempus is a substantial gallery—reasonable cash flow, a good client list, and a strong artist base. Customers know me. They know I'm a good artist myself, so they trust my advice. I plan to try to borrow $150,000 to buy in as a partner." I realized I was rambling and stopped.

"Not giving up your painting?"

"No, I'll always paint. My painting is going in a different direction now." *And maybe it's not as good as it used to be*, I thought. "It's different, but painting should evolve." I needed to change the subject, so I said, "I remember showing you a painting I'd done when I was ten."

"I remember it. It was of the ocean and the sculpture of the brass seals at Lovers Point Park in Pacific Grove."

"You took it seriously," I continued. "Not just the usual parental oohs and ahs, but comments on perspective, color, light, and composition. And you talked about how famous artists had dealt with those things." Embarrassed, I glanced around the gallery. "You took me seriously. I appreciate that."

He nodded.

After a while, he said he had to go. "Here's a birthday card for you." He handed me an envelope with my name written in his familiar, stylish handwriting.

"My birthday is in June."

He grinned. "I know. An early gift."

I watched him walk up the street until he disappeared in the pale sunlight.

At the apartment that evening, I worked on my current painting until almost two in the morning, then sat down with a glass of Cabernet. It was going well, but was taking much longer to paint than my previous paintings. Still, I was happy with it. Sitting in my chair looking at it, I realized that what I felt, maybe for the first time in my life, was contentment.

I opened the envelope from my father and found a Hallmark birthday card inside. I laughed out loud. A Hallmark card from my father. Inside the card was a check for $150,000 and a few words:

When I called Ellis to find out what hours you worked, he told me you were interested in becoming a partner. Be happy, work hard. ~Your father.

Chapter 7

I thought owning part of Tempus would make me feel even more satisfied, more content, but it did not. I spent all my time working at the gallery or thinking about what needed to be done at the gallery. My painting ground to a halt, which may not have been a bad thing, since I felt like I had lost my focus. When I attempted a painting now, I could not seem to let the brush lead me through to an emotion or a personality, or a place that my subconscious mind wanted to explore. The expressions on my figures' faces lacked the concentration I formerly could imbue them with. I started many paintings and abandoned them one by one. Sitting smoking a cigarette, staring at all my unfinished canvases, I felt sapped of energy. I set all of them aside and put my paints away.

It was Monday, the gallery was closed, and I had planned to meet with a young woman whose work I thought had real potential, but Ellis had informed me last night as we were closing up that he wanted to meet with her alone.

Fine with me. Hitting on young women artists was not his most attractive feature, but as long as he didn't hit on me, I wouldn't try to stop him.

I decided to phone my mother in Florida. I couldn't even remember the last time we'd talked.

The conversation was bland and superficial, which was what I had hoped it would be. She said she was glad I called and did not chastise me for not calling more often. But just as I was about to click off, my mother said, in a neutral tone, "The last round of treatments has not been particularly successful, I'm afraid. I should have discussed this with you before, Sarah, but I didn't want you to worry. I have had ovarian cancer for some time now. I've stopped chemo therapy."

I was shocked into monosyllables for a moment. Then she said a cheerful goodbye, and our conversation was over.

I paced, smoked a couple of cigarettes, left a message for Ellis that I needed a few days off, starting tomorrow. He wouldn't like it, but we had a good show hung that would stay up for another four weeks, so it was not a bad time to take a few days off.

I made arrangements to fly to Florida.

Driving my rental car down Sixteenth Street, dread and nervousness began building inside me. I turned on Bayou Boulevard and pulled into the familiar driveway. I hauled my carry-on out of the back seat of the car and stood for a moment. The immaculate lawns, the clean street, the pastel houses, and the silence were as I remembered them. I went to the front door and rang the bell. My father let me in.

"Hello, Sarah." He put his old confidence into his voice, for my benefit I'm sure.

But he was different, pale and thin. His clothes were different too. He was wearing an American sports jacket, a pale-blue shirt, no tie, gray slacks, and loafers. No more conservative European suits, expensive ties, and polished black Italian shoes.

"The housekeeper has your old room made up for you," he told me. "I'm glad you are here."

"Thanks." We both stood there in the entry under the gaze of an original Miró painting, neither of us saying anything, because we had nothing to say to each other.

I put my things away and came out to the airy two-level family room. "Any change…?" I assayed.

He shook his head. "The cancer has metastasized, I'm afraid. But the morphine is working. I believe she feels little pain," he said slowly. "The morphine deadens pain, but it makes her lethargic, and often relatively unresponsive. But she can converse for short periods." He tried a smile. "She will be glad you are here."

My eyes filled with tears. "She's in the bedroom?"

He nodded, and I went down the hall to her bedroom. A hospital bed and various bits of medical equipment were cold and intrusive in the bright, floral-themed room. I could barely recognize the withered figure with the neatly combed hair as my mother. Her eyes were closed. I had to retreat to her bathroom for tissues to blot up the tears streaming out of my eyes.

I can't do this. I can't keep this death-watch. But then I told myself, *Yes you can, you have to, it's all anyone can do.*

But it was also nothing. You sit and wait. I read parts of books I pulled off the living room shelves at random. I would occasionally go past my mother's bedroom door and see my father sitting by her bedside. I eavesdropped shamelessly from the hall. He was recounting their early days together—as much to himself as to her, because by then she was seldom conscious—stories of when they had first been married, and even before they had married.

He came out of her room crying, passed me without a word, and went to his bedroom.

Late one afternoon I went into my mother's room, the room glowing with the yellow roses she had always been fond of. I sat in the chair near her bed. She lay with her eyes closed. I checked the morphine pump, and it was at the setting the nurse said it should be. My mother opened her eyes and after a moment focused on me. I smiled and leaned close to hear her whisper, "Lisa…"

I pulled back, shocked. Her eyes closed, and she said nothing more. Her breathing continued fast and shallow.

After a moment I turned to go. My father was standing in the doorway. He started to say something to me, but I pushed past him, got in my car, and drove to Madeira Beach. I took off my shoes and wandered along the sand, my feet in the warm Gulf water. Far out on the western horizon, lightning flicked in the heart of a dark thunderstorm.

Sometimes I wish I was Lisa. She is past feeling pain now.

My father was sitting in the living room reading when I returned. "Don't feel remorse, Sarah, please. Dying people become disoriented. They lose interest in all the things that had been important to them in their lives. I heard her say 'Lisa,' but it means nothing. Her mind is not clear."

"Mother wanted Lisa with her in Florida, not me."

"She wanted the four of us to be together. But she could not live in Geneva, and little Lisa was so upset over our separation that to express her anger and hurt she insisted on staying with me in Geneva. You went with your mother. You helped her."

There was much correspondence for my father. The housekeeper piled it on the desk in the corner of the living room. I saw many University of Missouri return addresses and a few overseas postmarks. He spent hours each day answering them. He had a secretary come in for two hours a day. He had a script he would modify for each person. Then the secretary would take the day's bundle of letters away to be mailed. The language of loss and grief is so over-used and so meaningless. But what else is there?

I would often retreat to my old room to sit, sometimes cry. Not just for my mother, but for me, for all four of us, who had somehow drifted far away from each other. I lived in a daze, feeling nothing but dread for the death we all knew was soon coming.

The house was beautifully decorated, in perfect order, clean and unchanged from what I remembered. The air conditioning softly purred; rainbows shimmered in the spray of the lawn sprinklers in the immaculate lawn; the maid service came in to clean house twice a week. The cook came in twice a day to make meals. Nothing had changed since I lived there in my high school days.

I wandered the house, remembering those empty days. Most weekends I would go with Mother to a luncheon with her friends whose faces I could not remember. We would leave this air-conditioned house, drive in an air-conditioned car, sit in an air-conditioned restaurant talking about nothing, and then return to this silent house. A hermetic existence.

I had always thought that my time with Mother had brought us a bit closer together. But I'm not sure it did. In those days both of us were rather silent people. I think something of my mother had disappeared when she left Geneva.

Her best days—our best days—were when the four of us lived in Monterey. Mother had been a part of our lives then. She had been able to push back the darkness that lurked inside Father and Lisa and me. But when we moved to gray Geneva, our darkness overwhelmed her.

The summer before I left for NYU I would often see my mother standing in the silent air-conditioned living room of this house looking out the front window at the perfect lawn. I hated to see her so silent. I wanted her to change, but I made no effort to help her; instead I ran away to New York and buried myself in my art classes.

"We need to talk about the things in this house," my father said at breakfast. I had been there four days, and I knew my mother would not last more than another day or two.

The cook had laid out a beautiful breakfast on the table in the lanai under the black-and-white striped awning by the swimming pool. "If there are things you want to keep, let me know." He looked at the blue pool water. "I plan to sell this house."

I nodded. I liked that he had put back on his professional persona. His well-modulated voice, always one of his best features, inspired confidence.

"I won't be taking much," he continued. "Your mother and I accumulated very few things in our years together. She had this house professionally decorated, so I will have the things in it auctioned. She has made a list of all the specific items she wanted to go to someone, or to a certain charity. She gave me all the books, which I will have shipped to Missouri."

"You sound comfortably settled there."

He smiled. "I am. I like the town and the university." He smiled again. "And I think the university likes me. It helps that I donated a sizeable sum to them."

He rubbed his hand on the white plastic arm of the chair. "Among your mother's things, I see no paintings by you."

I stared at the lazy blue water undulating in the morning sunlight.

"No. I sent her none. I didn't think they would appeal to her."

My father nodded. I had never sent him one of my paintings either. "I'm hoping you'll come to visit me in Missouri sometime," he said.

"Yes, I will," I said without hesitation.

I wandered around the house again, the house I had always thought of as Mother's house. There were many beautiful objects in it, but none of them were of interest to me. My old bedroom seemed particularly bare. I guess she'd left it the way I'd left it when I went to New York. And I had never been an accumulator either.

Mother's jewelry box was open on the dining room table for inventory. I picked a silver necklace out of it.

That evening the cook had another wonderful, and wonderfully light, dinner prepared for us. "There is a piece of Mother's jewelry that I'd like to have. A necklace with silver chain and a topaz set in silver."

He smiled. "I remember that necklace. We picked it out together, you and I, a birthday gift for your mother. It was at that little jewelry store on Alvarado Street in Monterey."

My tears began again. I set down my utensils and waited for them to subside. When I had regained control, I told him, "Sometimes I feel like life is nothing more than a series of goodbyes."

"It's not. It's a story, with sorrow and joy and all the other emotions people feel. And in memory we can make the story whatever we want it to be."

I ventured into Mother's bedroom from time to time and looked at her gaunt face on the white pillow. Tears poured from my eyes; I could say nothing. She was beyond hearing or seeing me, and all the memories she had of me and of father and of Lisa she could no longer call to mind. For her we had ceased to exist.

The next afternoon just after lunch, I was sitting in the family room attempting to read Daphne du Maurier's book *My Cousin Rachel* without absorbing any of it.

Father was at his desk. The secretary had just left.

The day-shift nurse came into the room silently, her arms at her sides and her expression apprehensive.

Father looked up; we both knew what she was about to say.

"She is gone. I'm sorry."

Father and I filed into Mother's bedroom and stood silently by the bed. I touched the still hand on the floral bedspread once, then left the room. In the living room I resumed my seat and sat staring at my book for want of anything else to do.

Father notified his secretary to send out the note he had already written announcing my mother's death. He phoned the doctor and the funeral home.

Soon the funeral home people arrived with a stretcher to take my mother's body to the crematorium. My father, the attending doctor, the day nurse, and two stretcher-bearers disappeared down the hall. I tried to ignore the muffled conversation. The doctor reminded my father "…her ring," and I pictured the wedding band my mother had continued to wear even after the divorce. I set my book down and covered my face as tears burst out of me. Then I retreated to the poolside and sat under the striped awning hoping the gentle draft of the fan and the sun's flicker on blue water would burn my sorrow away. But they did not.

Eventually I heard the vehicles drive away.

The next day my father, in his professional persona, graciously met and chatted with Mother's friends, who came in little groups to pay respects.

I could do little but sit and shake hands and mope and wander the house. My father was friendly, welcoming, almost too solicitous.

But after people had gone and the cook had set dinner for the two of us and the house was still, he became a silent unsmiling ghost.

I ate quickly and left the house to drive around aimlessly for a while.

The next morning I walked Madeira Beach at first light. The gray dawn light, the delicious feel of the warm Gulf air soothed me. I walked along the water's edge. I'm sure my expression was as inwardly focused as the knotted expressions on the faces of the joggers that trotted past.

Arrangements for cremation had already been made. A brass urn containing ashes was later delivered to the house. I have no idea what my father did with it. It didn't matter. Mother had permanently disappeared from our lives.

The next day there was another "reception" at the house. The caterers did a beautiful job; a larger crowd came this time. I knew no one. My father resumed his public persona and spoke with everyone individually, thanking them for being part of my mother's life. The event went well.

The following morning I sat in a chair by the pool staring at a book I'd chosen at random, waiting to leave for the airport and my flight back to New York. Finally lunch was over and it was time for me to go.

I tiptoed into my mother's room—now cleaned, the medical equipment removed, the bed changed and made, the drapes open to the sunshine outside. Fresh yellow roses in a crystal vase. The whiteness, the emptiness, tore at my heart.

"Goodbye," I whispered, then I rushed out of the room through the familiar house and collected my suitcase.

"I'm leaving now," I called to my father. Then I went out into the bright white Florida sunshine to my rental car, where I sat mopping my tears while the air conditioner cooled the car.

My father came out of the house and stood in the front doorway, his hand raised in farewell. I managed to wave, then drove to Tampa Airport and caught my flight back to New York.

I had the flight attendant bring me four Bushmills, which I drank stolidly one after the other as the plane bored its way north to LaGuardia.

"Too late to ever know her," I whispered to the amber whiskey. "She is gone."

This undemanding woman who bore the anguish of all our desertions with dignity. *I can't fault her*, I thought. *She eventually gave up trying to dispel our darkness and retreated to the comfort of a few friends and a quiet life in the town where she had grown up.*

I wept bitter tears that night.

Next morning I sat in the rumpled sofa-bed in my apartment staring at my empty easel, remembering the row of art books on the bottom shelf of the bookcase in Mother's house. My senior year in high school, I had found my life in those books.

I got up, made coffee, and dressed. I stood feeling the warmth of the cup, got out my paints, set a clean canvas in place, and set to work.

I saw my mother as she had been in my high school days, standing before the big picture window in the living room, staring out at the perfect lawn, empty street, and pastel houses. Her auburn hair was always perfectly set. She dressed stylishly but not ostentatiously. I remembered walking past one day as she stood at the window. I could see just the faintest reflection of her face in the glass—not smiling, not frowning, something in between.

It took me three evenings to paint that image of my mother. While I worked to create her image, I felt the numbing emptiness to which she had been consigned and in which she would now always be.

When the painting was finished I put it away and showed it to no one.

Chapter 8

Working at Tempus kept my mind occupied. I was glad for that. It kept me from brooding too much about Mother's death. I did no painting for a week after I finished my portrait of my mother.

But then after a day of dealing with a troublesome client and arguing with Ellis over the design of the next exhibition, I sat in my apartment for a while staring at my easel, then set a canvas on it and started a maroon and green abstract and worked on it until two a.m.

This became an every-night occurrence. Painting reenergized me, and the paintings seemed to flow out of me without effort. No longer so large or so raw as they had been in my "second phase" (my after-Achille phase). My paintings were still very bold but now less aggressive, more poignant. I found I wanted to work with smaller canvases; my palette changed from red and black to maroon and iridescent green along with several shades of violet. Almost-humanoid abstractions came off my brush in postures of supplication, of penitence, of longing, of defiance.

One morning Ellis dropped by my apartment.

He was smiling, which appeared to pain him some. "Your stuff is selling as fast as I can hang it on the wall. You've got a following now, a real following, people with money."

I tipped back a slug of Bushmills whiskey. It was ten in the morning, and I had just gotten up after my usual session of painting until two a.m. I did not feel like talking, so he looked through my most recent paintings, then gave his typical little sigh and departed. I put the check he'd brought me in the desk drawer and tried to continue painting, but I was exhausted, so I cleaned my brushes and tumbled onto the couch, wrapping the comforter around me. I'd get up a little after noon and be at the gallery by two.

The phone rang, and I made the mistake of answering it. It was my father.

"I'm hoping you might take time away from your painting and your gallery to spend a day or two here in Columbia. Sometime soon."

Caught off balance, I agreed. The next few days I fought the urge to call him back and tell him I couldn't make it. Instead, a week later I told Ellis I needed a few days off and booked a flight to St. Louis.

I was a bit nervous on my first visit to my father. We each liked our own space, we were comfortable being alone, but... maybe now it was time to reconnect.

I had a rental car and drove from the airport to his house. I needed the car, needed the sense of freedom, in case it got too claustrophobic in his house with him. I don't keep a car in New York City, so it felt strange driving. But it was fun. Sort of like touring some quaint village in the Alps. The people in the big Midwestern houses I passed, all living their prosaic lives.

At the house, my father welcomed me in. I put my suitcase in the guest room and asked for a glass of wine.

"Little early, but I'll see what I've got." He rummaged around the little wine rack built into the space beside the refrigerator. "I think you'll like this Pinot." He poured me a glass.

I raised my glass. "To seeing you again," I toasted him.

He smiled that becoming smile so easy to mistake for warmth. "I'm glad you came, Sarah."

The wine was excellent—an Argo Pinot noir.

I found I enjoyed being there doing nothing. My father and I were polite to the point of formality with each other, but even that felt fine to me.

I walked around outside by myself a good bit. I read and helped him with errands, although at one point a small woman with a wide smiling face and perfect white hair dropped by to see if there was anything we needed.

My father introduced her as, "Cecelia. A neighbor."

We shook hands, my father assured her there was nothing we needed, and she departed.

I could see she was more than just a friendly neighbor.

On the flight back, concerns about the gallery immediately flooded back into my mind. I drank a couple of Bushmills and started making lists. But some of the serenity I had gained from my visit to Columbia stayed with me. I set my lists aside and daydreamed about another visit, perhaps in six months. And that became my routine for the next few years, perhaps the best years for Father and me. I would visit him for a few days each spring and a few days each fall.

Each visit was more enjoyable, in its low-key way, than the one before. My father and I learned how to be comfortable in each other's presence. His position as an adjunct economics professor at the University of Missouri clearly suited him. His endowment to the university and his eminence in the field, though sullied by his hasty departure from Eurovest, gave him the freedom to do the research he wanted to do. He had become a different person.

Neither he nor I had ever been fond of expansive shows of emotion. That false bonhomie, that Disney-flavored, sugar-coated nonsense seemed far more artificial to me than our rather distant affection.

We relied on routine to be sure everything would go well.

And for a couple of years he seemed unchanged each time I visited. He had settled into his place in this small town, this university. Similarly, I had settled into my place in New York, selling art, working and painting—though no longer frenetically, and always focused on the next canvas and the next.

After a rather stormy conversation with Ellis, I cashed out of Tempus and used the money to start my own gallery, which I named Aeroptix. It had not occurred to me to discuss my plan with my father. Only on a visit six months after I'd bought the gallery did it occur to me to tell my father.

My father and I sat in the old wood chairs at the long table in his backyard. The spring breeze was mild on the skin, and the sun seemed to make his backyard the land where it is always afternoon. I realized he had spoken to me.

"I'm sorry. What did you say?"

"I said you seem a bit preoccupied this morning, but you seem to have relaxed."

"A phone call this morning. Some business back in New York. Nothing." I sipped my good old Argo Pinot noir. "I just opened my own gallery."

He nodded. "Sounds like the right thing to do. When you were here last fall you were quite unhappy with the situation at Tempus Gallery."

"I was. I have worked hard there. By the way, thanks for the money to buy my partnership there. That rainy afternoon in New York when we met for a few minutes at the little café across from the front doors of the Met Art Gallery."

"Sounds to me like you've used it well. You appear to have built up Tempus's business considerably."

"I have. Revenue is now three times what it was when I bought it. And it's due mostly to me—my hard work and my art—and some lucky bets on a couple of other artists."

"So now you've sold your partnership." He touched his wineglass but didn't drink any of it. I noticed once again how mottled the backs of his hands were. No longer the handsome workingman's hands I remembered.

When we both were younger.

"I made a profit on my partnership. And once Ellis gets over his snit about me leaving Tempus, he'll actually be glad I've moved on. Things have not been pleasant between us for a while. It was time for me to move on."

"I assume your gallery is also on the Lower East Side."

"Yes. I hired an assistant. We've been open a month, and she seems to be good. But I need to get back. I'm flying back tomorrow morning. Sorry, I should have told you."

He nodded. "Quite all right."

For a moment I thought of inviting him to our grand opening next week. But I didn't. The smooth spring air, the silence of his backyard, the peacefulness of this tiny town all conspired against me trying to mix the two worlds. I like a compartmentalized life, I told myself. But on the flight back, a Bushmills in front of me, I wondered if the real reason might not be that I didn't want to risk failure in front of him.

I needn't have worried. The Aeroptix grand opening was a huge success. I had the place entirely decorated in red and white. Enough liquor and canapés even for the voracious art crowd, and invitations to literally everyone I knew in New York. And twice that number showed up.

It was three a.m. by the time the musicians had packed up and my people had swept up, and the caterer had the rented furniture stacked and tablecloths bundling all the leftover food and plastic glassware.

I waved to Steph, my assistant. "Good night, and thanks. See you tomorrow."

At home I locked the locks on the door and collapsed in the chair. Soon I was asleep. The next morning, while waiting for the aspirin to ease my hangover, I sat, coffee cup in hand at my usual window seat, staring out the gray window at the gray sky.

I'd hung all my paintings that I thought were any good for last night's grand opening. I hadn't painted anything new that was worthwhile in a long time.

I'd sunk every cent I had into an art gallery that would now take up all my time, so the paintings on the wall at the gallery were probably the last ones I'd do for quite a while. I had my lease on this rat-hole apartment and $100 K in the bank, which I was sure I'd run through in a year to get my gallery up and running.

And each evening I came home to an empty apartment.

Within a year of opening Aeroptix, my enthusiasm had waned. I kept this feeling suppressed in New York, where I slogged along day after day, my attention absorbed in the minutia of running a gallery.

On my next visit to Missouri, I uncharacteristically mentioned my loss of enthusiasm for my gallery. "Activities I once enjoyed are now drudgery." I smiled a little. "It takes a trip to Missouri to re-energize myself."

My father nodded, maintaining his Buddha-like smile. "Sometimes a little distance is a good thing." I let that double entendre pass. But I said no more about me. He took up the conversation smoothly, as always. "Just before I retired from the university, my colleagues and I completed a rather interesting project."

"Oh?" I asked politely.

"Re-evaluating the structure of regulated monopolies in the global economy." He laughed. "I can tell by your expression you find the subject intriguing."

I'd grown to enjoy his small town, walking the nearby campus, talking with him about familiar things, just as we had when I was ten years old and we would walk down the hiking path along the coast when we lived in Pacific Grove.

I liked our routine. Our conversations had developed and sculpted the personas we presented to each other. I loved the routine of my visits, the changeless feel of his house. The calm pleasure of morning coffee together, trivial conversations about our plans for the day. I had come to accept his friend Cecelia. She liked to be called Cece. The three of us now had brunch, which Cece fixed, at my father's house every Sunday I was in town.

I wanted my visits and our conversations to go on forever, unchanging.

When I began my visits, I had worried that living alone would not be safe for him as he aged. But it did not take me long to understand how much Cece cared for him, in all senses of the word. And she seemed to me to be completely trustworthy. In any case, she had my phone number and I had hers.

At one of our Sunday brunches Cece mentioned my father's novels.

"*Heart* was sort of a sequel to *Mosaic*," he said, smiling at Cece. "Also set in Geneva, but with some bits of Milan and Lugano as additional backdrop.

I wanted to try better to capture the personalities of the people in Switzerland and northern Italy. And of course international finance. Before my memories fade." He chuckled. "If Paul Erdman can do it, I can do it. I didn't even have to go to jail."

I had no idea who Paul Erdman was, so I said nothing. But I was unhappy that my father was using his past, my past, in books he was discussing with Cece. Publishing something for strangers was one thing, but bringing her into our lives felt intrusive.

I tried to explain some of this to him one evening, but he said it was simply discussing the stories with a friend. "She doesn't give advice about the story, just the writing style."

I stopped short of trying to tell him that those cities, the memories of us being there, were a part of my life that I didn't really want him to share with Cece. "I'm sorry," I told him. "Cece is a fine person, but I can't help feeling…exposed…when so much of these stories seem to be taken from a past that is still alive in my memory."

"I hope never to offend you, Sarah. But writing these books is a way of reliving the past, and perhaps saying goodbye to it," he told me with a gentle smile. "My memory is imperfect. Perhaps you could take these stories as an affirmation that these memories have value."

I made noncommittal sounds of agreement, but I was not placated. I left for New York wondering what should be done about this and finding no clear solution.

Back in New York, I started three canvases and quickly stalled. They sat staring at me for a week. Then one day—a particularly long and tiresome day at the gallery, arranging for the next show and telling my employees what I expected them to do—I came home, took a fortifying shot of Bushmills, deliberately painted over all three canvases, and put my paints away.

From then on I spent every day at the gallery, all day. But I still felt a restlessness that could not be satisfied. I tried taking an evening course in art evaluation that City University was holding, but I quit after two sessions, which cost me almost $800. I knew more than the instructor about how to evaluate new art.

My attitude toward my employees and toward new painters who auditioned to show their work in my gallery was cold, even by New York standards.

I was drinking less, which would have been good if I hadn't felt a restlessness that I could not put a name to. Alcohol, or lack of it, made no difference. But soon it was autumn, and I scheduled a visit to my father.

September fourteenth was Father's birthday. Cece had phoned me and told me she had planned a lunch for him and wanted to be sure I arrived in Columbia in time to attend it.

I arrived late the night before; my flight was delayed. My father had already retired for the night but had left the light at the front door on, which made me smile. I went in and closed the door behind me with a familiar double click.

When I woke, an autumn dawn was outlining the closed drapes in pale pink and white. The guest room was unchanged since I'd first started visiting: the plain white walls, a nice palette-knife painting of gladiolas on the wall opposite the bed. I put my clothing and suitcase in the closet when I came on visits, so the room always looked bare as a hotel room. But the sound of my father in the kitchen, the scent of the house and the clean sheets, sent a message to my unconscious: I was home. I lay there for a time, my mind emptying itself of all scurrying New York thoughts.

Like a patient woodworker shaping and smoothing a piece of wood, my visits here, our conversations, had brought me closer to my father, however little I truly knew him.

I joined my father in the kitchen, where we sipped coffee in silence. As I had walked into the brightly lit kitchen, the white of his hair, the narrowness of his neck, and the way his old sweater hung on his scrawny body made me feel very sad. But he seemed cheerful.

He smiled gently at me. "Looks like it will be a nice day."

"I plan to take a walk this morning, after I make us some breakfast," I told him. He nodded and moved to the living room and sat watching the morning light on the brick wall.

I stayed at the kitchen table, sipping the coffee, inhaling its scent, keeping my mind clear and empty as long as I could. Then I made bacon and eggs and toast topped with Cece's wonderful homemade marmalade.

Over breakfast, I told my father, "I'm painting far fewer canvases now than I was. Running the gallery devours my time. But the last few paintings I've done are smaller, and the color palette is softer. My style has changed." I didn't mention that those paintings had been done nearly two years ago.

"You sound like you are comfortable with your change of style."

"I am. My older stuff was so harsh, so dark, and so big, it wore me out. I can't do it like that anymore. After breakfast I'm going for a long walk—the day looks beautiful."

"Be back in time for lunch," my father told me as I left for my walk. "There is a surprise party for me at one o'clock." He laughed.

My father appeared to enjoy his birthday party, and I surprised myself by enjoying it too.

The lunch was quite nice. Cecelia and her friend Joan choreographed the event. Someone brought hand-rolled rigatoni that was as good as the stuff in the restaurants in Milan.

An arugula salad, fresh sourdough bread from the local bakery, and four different kinds of olives— Cecelia set the bowls triumphantly on the table. "There. Very Mediterranean." The sunshine was pale, the day still and mild. My father drank two glasses of a Monterey Beaujolais someone had brought. He reminisced about his last year at the university to an occasional boisterous laugh from everyone at the table. He was once again quite the raconteur. I tried to remember some of the stories he used to tell me as we walked the bike path in Monterey, but I could remember none of the specifics, only that I was hugely entertained by them.

The people at the table were clearly fond of him, although I knew that people often misread his engaging exterior as warmth. But he was very definitely a charismatic person. Able to keep a conversation going without monopolizing it, and to make everyone feel included. I remember him once telling me the hardest part of his work at Eurovest had not been formulating the plan, but in achieving consensus on it.

I wandered into the kitchen, poured myself a glass of Pinot, then went to the living room to peruse his bookcase once again. I pulled out one of the novels he'd written: *Mosaic*. It had not sold well, Cece had told me. She quoted a critic as saying my father made the European settings real, but the people did not come alive. I thumbed through it but found it too dense with characters, so I slid it back into its place on the shelf. *He won't write any more. He is frail now. What would I do if responsibility for his health, his life, fell to me?* I had a little money in the bank, but not much. I certainly couldn't come to Missouri and care for him. My life was in New York.

When the party ended, people cleared the table with Midwestern efficiency. The last to leave was Cece. Father thanked her profusely for the party.

It was one of those perfect autumn afternoons—sunny, cool, and still. The orange and yellow leaves on the trees and the green of the ivy on the brick wall in the backyard was beautiful in this light. The colors of a Vermeer.

He set his glass aside. "How about a walk?" This was a common ritual during my visits.

I slipped on a sweater, and we set out. I started out briskly but slowed when I found he was walking much more slowly.

"Going to have to go slow I'm afraid."

"Is anything wrong?"

He shook his head. "No, I just don't feel as well as I used to, that's all. Nothing to worry about."

The sidewalk was colored by fallen maple and oak leaves. We could hear an occasional football game from television sets inside the houses we passed. As always, we walked straight down his block and three more blocks to the university campus. The brick homes in his neighborhood were large, old, and well cared for.

We passed only a few people, strolling like us in the afternoon sun.

I never know whether to greet strangers I pass on the sidewalk in the Midwest. In New York, you don't greet anyone, but here many people greet perfect strangers as they pass. For me, that quickly gets tiresome and hollow.

Down the long gray sidewalk, a young woman walked toward us briskly, swinging one arm more than the other. She was dressed in a bulky sweater, jeans tucked into leather boots, light-brown hair pulled back in a short ponytail. We greeted her as she approached, and she smiled quickly and said hello. She wore glasses with large, dark frames.

She passed us with a purposeful stride, eyes averted.

"She reminds me of you," he commented, "your first year at NYU. I worried about you a little then. You pushed yourself quite hard. Perhaps you still do."

We reached campus and walked between the brick buildings to the quadrangle with its tall oak trees. As we walked around the quad in silence, I knew my father was rerunning his internal video of the year he had met my mother. They'd met in this little college town right here on this campus.

We slowly made our way back along the four blocks from campus to his house. A man was out in his yard mulching a flowerbed, and my father greeted him. The air was crystalline with the breathless fragility of Indian summer.

I found myself trying not to notice how much he had aged. His arms were thin, his gait unsteady. He did not much resemble the smiling confident man he had been, the man in the photo albums on the bottom shelf of the living room bookcase.

"Have you noticed how silent the days are in the fall?" he said as we reached the house. "All the birds have flown south and there are no more summer insects. We don't notice what is all around us until it is gone."

Chapter 9

I stood shivering in the January Missouri wind, wondering what was taking him so long, but eventually my father opened the door of his house and welcomed me in. He looked very old and frail. But I held on to my smile, hauled my suitcase inside, and closed the door.

"Hi," I said, hoping I didn't sound too falsely hearty. Cecelia was there.

I went down the familiar hall, put my suitcase and coat in the guest bedroom, and joined them in the kitchen where Cecelia had laid out teacups, saucers, and a sugar bowl. I was resentful she used my mother's Noritake china, but I put a smile on my face and said, "You are looking well, both of you."

"Tea?" Cecelia asked, raising the pot.

"I think I'd rather have a glass of wine."

I poured myself a generous measure out of an open bottle of Argo Pinot noir. I still marveled at my father's ability to find this great Pinot in this tiny university town, while I couldn't seem to find anything nearly as good in New York City for even double the price.

"I can drive up to the store," I volunteered. "Get some food for dinner, but I need to go soon. The rain is freezing and the streets are getting slick."

"No need," Cecelia said. "I brought a small welcome-home dinner for you two. I'll drink my tea and walk home. I walk across the lawns instead of on the slippery sidewalk."

She opened a wicker hamper and began laying out small plates, beautifully prepared, on black Mikasa china.

"This is very gracious of you, Cece," I said, topping up my wine glass with what I hoped was a warm smile.

She beamed at me and at my father, who was sitting in meditative silence.

"It's good to see you again, Sarah." She finished her arrangements, flashing me a glance from her extraordinary blue eyes. "I'll leave you two to talk. I need to be on my way."

"Be careful," my father warned as he accompanied her to the door.

"She lives quite nearby," he said, seeming to need to reassure me of Cece's safety.

We sat down to the meal Cece had brought and talked of inconsequential things. This was the ritualized beginning of all my visits, conversations meant to let us settle once again into each other's company. Conversation both casual and yet as formalized as a

Kabuki play. Familiar stories of the past: Christmas at Zermatt, walking the bikepath Saturday mornings in Monterey, fond memories burnished by telling and retelling

He brightened as we ate and talked, displaying the wit an articulateness I had admired since I was a child.

I did not mention that Cecelia had phoned me three days ago voicing concern over his health.

"He's not old, but he acts like he is. I see troublesome signs of withdrawal," she'd told me. "He naps a lot and lapses into long silences. I'm sure a visit from you will help restore his spirits."

After we finished the flan, I loaded the dishwasher while my father shuffled out to the living room.

I brought two glasses of Pinot to the living room, where he had taken his usual seat in the reading chair near the window.

The low-voltage garden lights were on, making the ice-crusted grass glitter. I slipped off my shoes and curled my feet under me on the old sofa. His face in the pale glow above the reading light looked calm, confident, and familiar. I loved moments just like these: the quiet house was its own cozy little world.

Despite the good bit of effort it had taken us, I felt like we now had a mature, even loving, relationship. Like all children who feel they may be reaching parity with a successful parent, I wanted this equality to go on forever, never changing. But he had aged significantly in the last year, and along with age had come sorrow, and a touch of bitterness.

"I read the book about you and Eurovest," I told him. "*Horizons*, I think it's called, by Haldor somebody. At least I read the chapter about the years when you were chief of policy division."

"Don't take Haldor's words too seriously. He was working under a grant from the finance division of the EU, and they had very specific requirements for his history of Eurovest."

"Which was?"

"To ensure Eurovest was seen in the best light possible."

"He seems to have met those requirements. You and your colleagues at Eurovest seem to have accomplished a great deal."

"For a while we did."

I sipped my wine. "You could have shared those successes with me."

His face looked very old in the lamp shadow. "Why? You were in New York, involved with your art." He went on, "You had your own life."

He got to his feet slowly and shuffled down the hallway to the bathroom again.

"And I chose to go back to New York after Lisa died," I said to the empty room. I went to the kitchen, refilled my glass, and returned to the living room. *I put Lisa out of my mind, and I put Achille and Mother out of my life. I concentrated on my painting. Self-centered, but perhaps that's the price of success. The paintings I did then, in the period after Lisa died, are among the strongest paintings I have ever done. They made my reputation.*

I got down Father's book *Horizons* again and tried to find what he had been thinking in that period after Lisa's death, but there was nothing. It was as though Lisa and Mother and I did not exist.

He came into the room and silently resumed his chair, where he sat expressionless in the yellow lamplight.

"Can I get you a glass of wine? A cup of tea?" I asked.

He shook his head no.

"I didn't realize that you were next in line to become the director general of Eurovest," I said conversationally.

He frowned. "Yes. For a time I was the fair-haired boy there. It helped that I was an outsider—an American—because Switzerland, and the European financial community itself, is really a rather small place. The external pressures over strategic direction, the feuding personalities, the longstanding intercultural feuds..." He waved a bony hand. "I was able to avoid much of that. But still the pressure on me, on all of us in the policy division, was intense. The stakes were high. If we made a mistake, it could flatten a nation's economy for a time. Still, I flatter myself that I lead a team that produced much good work." He looked at me. "But I like it better here. A small university, where I work without pressure."

"Why didn't you ask mother to join you here?"

He turned his face to the window. "I have no answer to that question, Sarah. None you would understand." He rubbed his hands together. The room was warm enough, but the view of the accumulating ice outside made it seem cold.

"I thought we were better off apart," he said, looking at me as though asking for confirmation that he had been right. "Your mother and I talked by phone from time to time, but she no longer confided in me. I had no idea how fast her cancer was advancing..."

I felt my tears welling. He put a shadowy smile on his face. "Once I learned of her situation and flew to Florida, we did have time to ourselves for a while, a short while. For those few days the pain medication gave her a false energy, a kind of fragile brightness. We both knew that the tumors would grow and the pain medication would take her mind away, but we ignored that, lived in the past, and became the loving people we had been when we first met." His voice broke, then he resumed. "I reminded her of the two years I was in the army, distant from her, but very much in love with her. But I could usually get leave to spend a weekend with her every couple of months. We would have forty-eight hours together. We stayed at her apartment, saw no one, went nowhere, just lived to be with each other."

He rubbed his eyes. His hands, the strong workman's hands I had known my whole life, were now veined and gnarled. "Long ago, but very good times indeed."

"We've had good times. Recently," I said. "I think that we've come to understand each other and perhaps to feel the affection father and daughter should feel."

"Yes. I have always loved you, Sarah, though I don't demonstrate it well. Part of my distance was caused by my perception that you are strong and self-sufficient. You set out to become an artist and succeeded."

"That success seems to have faded," I said softly. "I haven't painted anything in a long time. But you set me on the road to gallery management, and for that I am grateful." I sipped my wine. "Although now my interest in gallery management has faded a bit." I tried to smile. "But I think I have made a success of it."

I don't think he heard me. He was concentrating on getting to his feet, holding on to the back of the chair. Then he made his way slowly down the corridor, his hand sliding along the wall. "I must retire now." His bedroom door closed. The house was silent.

I went to bed, but sleep eluded me. The clock said two when I got back up, went to the dark kitchen, and poured myself another glass of Pinot.

In the living room I brushed my fingers along the books on the shelf. Carlos Baker's biography of Hemingway; The *Alexandria Quartet* by Durrell; *The Magus* by John Fowles; poetry by Cavafy, Rossetti, and Robinson Jeffers.

I pulled out the Fowles book. "This is appropriate. The god game." The book fell open to the last page. My father had hand-written a translation of the last line, which Fowles wrote in Latin: *Let those love who have never loved before, and let those who have loved before, love again.*

I always enjoyed the beginning of *The Magus* and never read the middle. I sat down and started reading.

I woke up in my father's reading chair and found him leaning over me.

"Perhaps you should go to bed," he said.

I set *The Magus* aside. "I couldn't sleep."

"Nor can I. My sleep is very thin these days." He looked as though he was going to say more but didn't.

I moved to the couch, and he sat down in his chair. He stared out the window into the night for a time, then looked at me. "Lisa destroyed me."

My heart grew cold. "Brutal honesty is seldom helpful."

"And I think it was because she felt I was destroying her. It is not false modesty for me to say that work I was doing at Eurovest was very good. If I had had more time, I know it would have been brilliant." He shot me an interrogatory look. "Lisa wanted to be better than me."

"The ambition of many children," I said.

"But in her case, she took the wrong path."

"I could have done great things at Eurovest," he stated in his querulous old-man's voice. "But Lisa made that impossible."

Silence fell.

"After she died, I moved quickly to try to erase Lisa's financial scheming, but that failed. I enlisted

Achille's help, but that did not work either, and in fact only resulted in some harm to his reputation. But my memory has healed that painful time so thoroughly that I have little memory of it anymore. Achille suggested a memorial service for Lisa at St. Germaine Church, a church he attended when he was in Lugano. It was done quickly, more for the benefit of Lisa's friends and schoolmates at the Rossey School than for us." Shaking his head slowly, he continued his reflection. "Lisa always did like breaking the rules, taking chances, staying out late…all the rebellious things schoolgirls do."

I never did rebellious things, I thought.

"You were never that way, I'm happy to say. At the Rossey School Lisa seemed to settle down. I'd drive over to Davos every month or so to visit her. I talked with her about my work, including highly confidential matters relating to European central bank prime rate setting. She seemed interested." He looked at me, his face barely visible in the darkened room—ghostly. "That was a mistake. Lisa and a schoolmate of hers—a girl name Aurora Tessier, who happened to be the daughter of the director general of Credite Lyonesse—decided to capitalize on what I was telling Lisa. They opened a bank account in Monaco and used the rate change information they got from me to make substantial profits reselling loans on the Zurich Bourse with Credite Lyonesse's cooperation. They built up quite a small fortune, and helped Lyonesse make an even larger fortune."

"Two twenty-year-old girls?" I was amazed. But...I remembered the tough Lisa I had seen in New York, the rebel.

My father continued, "For her and Aurora it was a game. But they soon were found out. The director general of Eurovest, a German, ordered an audit of Lyonesse because he thought the French were doing something inappropriate..."

"But it was only Lisa and her friend..."

"Nothing was proved to be illegal. But the rules of confidentiality, of 'insider trading,' had definitely been broken. Things went badly then for me. For reasons that are inexplicable to me even now, I elected to try to cover up her wrongdoings. I should not have. And worse, I destroyed Achille's career by asking him to place some very precarious trading positions for me. That effort failed, and it cost him his license. I was encouraged to 'resign,' which I did, rather hastily. Aurora Tessier and her father at Credite Lyonesse took it all in stride. Credite Lyonesse was 'counseled' about profit taking, but Mr. Tessier was very well connected in French politics, and since a French bank had managed to take advantage of the German-dominated Eurovest, the French government stayed smugly silent. On the scale that Eurovest operated, the amounts of money involved were trifling, though they were millions of euros."

"I assume all this is in one of your novels?"

"Indirectly. I wanted to write about Lisa and expiate my guilt. But I found I could not. She is there, but it is not the real her. The real Lisa is missing. I wanted badly to talk with you when you and I met in Lugano, at the art museum. It was too late for all that had happened, but I felt rather lost, and…" He rubbed the arms of his chair. "But you could not hear me. You were distraught over leaving Achille, but you said nothing about his effort to help me. Apparently he had told you nothing about it."

"The Viaggio Museum," I said. "It was raining that day. I was standing in front of a Rembrandt." I paused. "Achille had told me nothing of all that you've just described. But it explains how tense and distracted he was at the time, though I'm ashamed to say, I was not sympathetic."

My father continued, "We went to the museum tea shop. You wanted to tell me about your dreams, about guilt over Lisa's death, about Achille and you and your inability to communicate with each other. I could see all that in your face. But we did not speak of it."

He leaned forward a bit, and the light lay along the side of his face, putting in white and black the face that I had resented and loved my entire life.

"I wanted to shield you from the truth."

"But now you don't." I drank down my wine. "I know now that Lisa and I demanded a degree of affection from you that no one could provide. I'm sorry we were that way."

"Let's forgive each other, alright? And by the way,

Achille recovered from the financial disaster. He lives in London now, I'm told," my father said. He got to his feet with some difficulty. "I must return to bed now," he said. One hand on the wall, he shuffled down the corridor to his bedroom.

The next morning I woke hung over, took some aspirin, and stumbled to the kitchen. The clouds were gone, the sun was shining, and the ice sparkled. It was beautiful, but I could not appreciate it. I just wanted to go—to get away from a past I no longer knew.

Apparently, the ever-helpful Cecelia had already come and gone. The coffee was ready, some toast sat in the toaster, poached eggs rested in their warmer, and two place settings of Mother's Noritake china were on the breakfast table.

I ate, went to my computer, and found a flight to New York leaving at two that afternoon.

About eleven o'clock I heard my father shuffling down the hallway. He was unshaven and looked worse than the night before. He mumbled a greeting to me, poured himself a cup of coffee, and sat at the kitchen table staring at the birds on the birdfeeder outside the kitchen window. He was only sixty, but he looked and acted like he was eighty.

I ate a second slice of toast with Cece's homemade marmalade. I told Father I needed to get back to New York today, in fact, right now.

He nodded, not shifting his gaze from his view of the birds. "I understand."

I packed quickly and found him at the front door holding himself up with one hand on the wall. I recognized the corduroy pants and a gray sweater he'd bought at a little shop in Cortina d'Ampezzo on a weekend trip the first year we lived in Geneva.

I stepped forward, and for the first time since I was ten years old, we hugged each other.

He stood in the doorway. "Sorry about so much truth last night. It seldom does much good, but I wanted to say it all just once. Now, let's get back to being happy."

I went out into the cold clear day and put my suitcase on the back seat. I started the car, got the heater going, and put the window down. I knew what he would say next, and he did.

"Be happy, work hard."

"I will," I told him.

As I turned the corner, I had a last glimpse of him standing in the brilliant morning sunlight, one hand raised in farewell.

Chapter 10

Back in New York, I buried myself in the business of running Aeroptix. I was tired of the paperwork, and when I was honest with myself, I was tired of everything to do with the gallery—the receptions, the meetings with artists who wanted me to show their work, the endless cozying up to clients to keep them coming back, taking old art down and hanging new art. I had worked hard, but all I saw in the future was more hard work.

The winter sales had been slower than usual, but now that spring had finally arrived, I told myself things would pick up.

One Sunday in April, I had the front door of the gallery open to the mild breeze coming up the streets from the East River. I was thinking of the familiar cadence of my father's footsteps on hardwood floors years ago at Tempus Gallery when he had stopped in to see me. It had been an early spring day much like this one.

My phone chimed, showing my father's Midwestern area code, and stupidly my heart surged for an instant. But it was Cecelia, sounding very strange.

"Bad news, I'm afraid," she said.

"My father…?"

"…died yesterday morning. About five o'clock."

"I see." I was stunned. My unconscious mind took over. "I'll fly out there tomorrow to make arrangements—"

"He was cremated this morning," Cecelia went on, in a voice that did not seem to be hers at all. "That was his wish."

I stared at the brownstone across the street, a banner fluttering in the spring breeze. Anger washed over me. "You had no right to do that…"

"His will stipulated that he be cremated immediately," Cecelia said, "which I have done."

"Without notifying me first?" My voice cracked.

Cecelia's voice became a whisper. "He named me executor."

"You?" I shouted. "Not me?"

Cecelia began crying, which angered me further, but I clamped down on my rage and apologized.

"He thought it would be easier on you this way," Cecelia said. "He left very specific instructions on those points."

"I'll be there tomorrow," I told her rather frostily. "I assume I can still stay in the house?"

"Of course," she said, momentarily regaining composure. "He willed the house to you."

Cecelia began to cry again.

"I'll be there tomorrow," I managed to say and clicked the phone off.

In the quiet of the gallery, I found myself listening for the sound of my father's footsteps on the hardwood floors.

I flew to Columbia and moved into the guest room at his house. He would have known he was dying when I paid my winter visit to him. But he'd said nothing. And despite his obvious frailty, I'd chosen to believe that we could go on as we were forever, sustaining the pleasant superficial happiness we had built up over these last years.

Grief is selfish. The first thing that came to my mind as I walked through the silent house was: *I am alone. My little sister is dead, my mother is dead, and now my father is gone. Only I am left.*

Then a flash of anger. *I had no idea he would die. Was he ill? He looked weak and old, but not ill.*

Despite my twice-yearly visits to him, which I had grown to look forward to a great deal, I had barely gotten to know him. Now that door had softly closed; the journey of our getting to know each other was ended.

My anger came back again, and tears. The time is gone!

"I guess I can stop worrying about you living alone now," I told the daffodils nodding in the springtime breeze outside the back window. "Now I guess I need to start worrying about me living alone." I poured a glass of Pinot and continued roaming restlessly through the house, talking to myself. "And making Cecelia executor of your will. What is that all about? You've once again excluded me."

But I was confident Cecelia would do a good job. She seemed honest and highly organized. "But I'm highly organized too," I told the quiet space of the guest room.

A note I found later said *…take it out of your hands so you won't be tempted to keep more of my things…*

"Damn it! I don't want the handling of your estate taken out of my hands. I want to be responsible."

Not that it mattered much. His friends, colleagues, and favorite charities had been carefully enumerated in his will. Cece, whom I spitefully continued calling Cecelia, insisted I confirm her accounting for all the financial transactions.

"This house is yours," she said. She'd laid all the papers out on the kitchen counter for me. "Here are the accounts. I've kept the utilities, the lawn service—everything is to continue just as it…was."

Which rather surprised me. I had fully expected he'd made arrangements for selling this house and everything in it before he died. I had heard him say more than once that keeping sentimental kitsch was pointless.

Cecelia raised her eyebrows when I expressed my surprise that he had left the house to me. "He felt a great deal of love for you, Sarah. But…" She glanced downward, then back up at me. "He kept much of himself inside, including his love for you. Leaving you this house and these books may have been his last effort to show that love."

I nodded. "Perhaps."

"But he was also decisive," Cece continued. "I don't think he discussed his personal plans with anyone. He just thought things through, then acted. I am as surprised as you that he made me executor of his will."

"He was very fond of you, I'm sure."

Her blue eyes turned to me. "I felt a great deal of affection for him," she said. "And I think we understood each other."

"Well, this is certainly a surprise," I said, fingering the folder with the deed to the house in it. "May cause a bit of difficulty since I've still got a lease on my gallery back in New York and I am the only full-time employee."

With a certain drama Cece opened a third folder.

Inside was a single sheet of paper, a bank statement from a Monaco bank, written in French. Cece pointed to a line. "Your father left you 6.2 million euros."

I stared at the paper. "He was certainly a man who liked his secrets," I said finally. "That's a lot of money."

"That should put your mind at ease about maintaining this house and operating your gallery in New York," Cece said. "I'll go now, let you get accustomed to all this. Unless you would like me to join you for lunch?"

I declined and she started out, but I caught her at the door. "I haven't really properly expressed my appreciation for all you've done, Cecelia. You've done a masterful job handling his affairs. I can't thank you enough." I touched her arm. "I hope he provided for you as well."

"He did." She smiled and walked away.

I wandered through the house, then back to the kitchen counter where the papers lay. After a while I put them on the desk in the guest room I was still using as my room. I found I was listening for the clomp of my father's footsteps down the hall. Listening for his voice from the other room—the polished enunciation, pauses, and emphases of an accomplished public speaker and hider of the truth.

I stopped my wandering in front of the bottle of Argo Pinot on the kitchen counter, poured myself a generous glass, and toasted my reflection in the black glass of the microwave.

Money in the bank.

I could go back to New York, hire more help at the gallery, and let this house sit here for a while. Or, I could do something else. But what?

Money from my father.

He had paid my way through NYU and provided a generous allowance for me for a number of years afterward. I'd never told Ellis that. I let him assume I was a starving artist like everyone else. My one-room apartment in New York certainly had not hinted at an independent income. I smiled at my wine—me hiding the truth, just like my father. And later my father gave me $150,000 to buy into Tempus, which had been very good for me for a while. Then I cashed out and bought Aeroptix. That had been good for a while too. But the last year it had all felt like I'd been doing the same thing for far too long. The fun had gone out of it.

The problem was, I wasn't sure what would be fun. Go back to New York and spend more time with my friends in Manhattan? Not likely. I had acquaintances by the dozen, but no friends. When I was painting I had no time for friends, and when I started managing galleries I had even less time. Ellis was maybe the closest I had to a friend. I knew he had recently cashed out of Tempus, but I'd lost track of him.

Ellis. I smiled, remembering his gangly walk, his foppish hair, his brusque manner. I filled up my wine glass and sat down in my father's chair to observe the light on the backyard hedge and brick wall. Ellis had given me my start. I never would have started selling at the prices I did if he hadn't been behind me, pushing me to paint the best I could and pushing clients to buy my work.

But I'd returned the favor, sort of. The years I managed Tempus were its best years. I was organized, knew art, and quickly learned how to deal with clients so they kept coming back and bringing other clients—new clients—with them. Word of mouth was the only thing that counted in the world of art sales in our price range in New York. And I knew how to spread that word of mouth. In a sense it was teaching clients how to view art.

I'd sold my partnership in Tempus Gallery for $400,000 (pretty reasonable growth from the $150,000 my father had given me to buy in), but I'd spent it all on Aeroptix, which I'd be lucky to sell for $200,000. "Rather ironic," I told myself. "I work my butt off running Aeroptix just to see my investment shrink by half." I shrugged. The wine was nice, even if my memories were not.

Who had I made myself into? I still lived in the same apartment I'd rented ever since I graduated from NYU. How long ago was that? My early paintings were still worth what people had paid for them. I kept track of art prices. All gallery owners had to. But those prices might fluctuate if I started painting again and offered new paintings to the market. It is strange economics, but paintings by a single artist tend to change value as a unit, not as individual paintings. The price could easily go down.

I doubted if anything I painted now would be worth nearly as much as my early work, since I had not felt that "fine fire" of my early paintings for a long time. In fact, I felt no fire about painting, running a gallery, or even returning to New York City.

All the excitement of selling my paintings for amounts that boggled my young mind, working with Astrid to build momentum in her galleries, flying back and forth from New York to Milan, Achille and me and the Villa Fiore. Working for Ellis at Tempus and seeing it prosper; later having my own gallery—it all seemed like another lifetime as I sat in this quiet Midwestern house. Had they been the best years of my life?

The flash and trash and the angst and exhilaration of total immersion in the New York art scene had sustained me for a long time. But not anymore. I did not know what I wanted next, but I did know one thing: I was finished with Aeroptix. I waited until noon, then phoned the last number I had for Ellis. I was surprised to hear him answer on the third ring.

"Sorry to wake you," I told him cheerily. "How would you like to buy a gallery?"

There was a long silence, then, "Aeroptix? You're quitting?"

"I prefer to call it moving on," I told him. "But yes, I'm offering Aeroptix to you. I haven't spoken to anyone else, and I'm willing to make you a great deal on it."

We talked for a while, and when I started talking price, his interest grew.

"I'll sell you the gallery lease for $200,000."

There was a long silence.

"I know it's worth a lot more than that, but I want to do you a favor. You helped me when I was starting out, so now I'm helping you."

He started babbling about start dates and contracts and leases, but I cut him off. "You can work all that out. I'll send you a limited power of attorney and you attend to the details. I trust you. But there is one condition."

Another long silence. "Oh?"

"I would like for you to ship all my paintings to me here at my father's house. All the stuff in my apartment. Just have a moving company go in there, pack everything, and ship it to the address I'll give you when I send you the power of attorney."

"You're leaving New York." Another long silence. Leaving New York permanently is inconceivable to people like Ellis.

"Yes. I'll be living here in Missouri for the foreseeable future."

But soon he got over his shock, agreed to my price, and agreed to ship me my paintings and the other stuff in my apartment.

I clicked the phone off feeling relieved but disoriented. I'd put the past behind me, but I didn't yet know which way to look for the future.

Chapter 11

June came to the Midwest with mild temperatures but dull, overcast skies and frequent rains. Even the summertime flowers and birds seemed a little dispirited. Despite the drizzle, I walked every afternoon. Here and there, up this block and down that, getting to know my father's town. To my surprise, I found I rather liked it.

Cece offered to help me go through my father's things, evidently assuming I'd find it a tearful ordeal, but I refused. Going through the books and papers in his study, the souvenirs in the living room, the books on the shelves, or the cookware and plates in the kitchen was an exploration of someone I had both known and never known. I was hungry to see him, reflected in his belongings. The books on the bookshelves had been in the same place, the same order, since I first began visiting him here.

Every few days Cece would make a very short, tentative visit, "just to lend a hand, if needed."

Sometimes I'd offer tea, which she would then make; sometimes, if my mind was elsewhere, I would offer nothing. She was good about not hanging around aimlessly. More than once, as we chatted about the town (her way of helping me learn where things were), the conversation would drift toward my father and I would detect a hint of emotion. One purpose of her visits was to ensure that I did not too hastily dismantle his arrangement of things in the house. For Cece and me, this house was his persona now that he was gone.

I felt no ambition besides my leisurely exploration of Father's house, strolls around campus, and walks around town in the summer heat.

Every day I would drift from room to room, touching books, art works, furniture, cookware. Every room but his bedroom, which was bare of everything. Once in a while I might advance a step or two into it, standing for a moment looking at the impressions of bed and chair on the cleaned carpet. Then I would retreat.

One afternoon when the rain was so heavy I decided to skip my walk, I made a cup of tea and opened one of the books he had published—a novel titled *The Elementary Language of the Heart*. It was set in Switzerland and concerned financial shenanigans, but there was nothing in it I found interesting. After a while I set it aside, grabbed an umbrella, and set off down the sidewalk at a fast pace.

An hour later, my feet soaked, I returned home, and after a hot shower I sat at the kitchen counter looking through the book again. Published the year before he died. Still nothing very interesting. Although on a blank page at the end of the book he had hand-written some lines from Cavafy:

...keep your destination, Ithaka, always in mind, but do not hurry the journey. When you arrive you will be rich with experience and you will find Ithaka much poorer than you remembered. She has nothing left to give you, but you are wealthy from the journey.

After a while I put the book back on the bookshelf. The rain had stopped, but the afternoon was dark.

I found a biography of him, poured myself a glass of wine, and started reading. But the book was a simplistic gloss about a happy American family of four living in Geneva. The facts were there, but the important points were never stated. No mention of Lisa's death or my parents' divorce. It ended with a recap of my father's career with Eurovest.

I went through all the books that he had written, or were written about him, and found a variety of hand-written notes.

In one book he had noted a date, *June 13th, 2000*, and below it a single line:

Christine passed away.

In another book he imperfectly quoted Christina Rossetti:

"…forget and smile, don't remember and cry."

And in another book I found what could have been a posthumous letter to me:

Memory is mutable, Sarah. I would like for you to remember me, your mother, and your sister, in a clear and loving light. Keep only the images that bring you joy, let the dark ones fade away.

"Now I'm alone," I whispered to myself one day. But I didn't feel lonely. Every day I walked the calm street from his house to campus and back. The same blocks he and I had walked together many times in sparkling autumn weather or breezy springtime.

I found another note of his: *…violated my own advice. I left you the house with many of my possessions still in it. Here's the reason: I'm hoping it will provide a memory anchor for you for a while. When you touch my old books, or look at the painting by Joan Miró, the one your mother liked so well, you'll get a feeling for who all four of us were in those bright years when we were all together and happy. You can restructure your memories and from them gain some insight into where you want to go. But if that's not what you want to do, I have no objection to you disposing of all of the objects in this house. I will have no further use for them (here's where we both laugh).*

But I was crying.

One day summer rain wakened me before dawn. I lay listening to the subdued patter, luxuriating in the small, comfortable bed in the guest room. Eventually I got up and, coffee in hand, sat reading and watching the morning light color the wet grass and the brick wall darkened by rain.

I felt no urgency to do anything. My father's bequest of money had provided me the freedom to do nothing. And for the moment that was exactly what I wanted to do. I felt guilty for not feeling guilty about doing nothing. All emotions seemed to have left me. I thought of my painting, the ferocity with which I attacked canvas after canvas in the early years and I could not recognize that person.

My boxes from New York arrived. I had the shipping company stack the boxes in the garage, where I opened them one by one. I barely glanced at my old, completed paintings. They were the ones I had considered second-rate and had not even offered for sale. Except for my painting of Mother and my painting of Lisa. I looked at the date on one of them and felt the guilt of time passing unused, but I didn't set up my easel and start painting. Instead I continued my lassitude, the humid summer days passing slowly like the clouds in the sky. I read from this book and that. Most days I would walk for hours, just like I had walked the beach at dawn when I was in high school.

Each day was the same as the last. I lived like a hermit, seeing no one, knowing no one, and wanting to know no one.

But maybe it was the physical presence of my painting gear and some of my old paintings that triggered my unconscious.

I went into my father's bare room and stood for a moment in the silence. *This will be my studio,* I thought. I unpacked my easel and set it up. After lunch I went to an art supply store and bought what I needed, set a canvas on the easel, and began a painting.

It was terrible.

But I resolutely tried another one and another. In the following days I reviewed some of my elementary art books from my high school days. I was starting all over again.

Leafing through the books was wonderfully nostalgic. A stamp on the inside cover read, *Haslam's Used Bookstore, Central Avenue, St. Petersburg, FLA.*

I wondered if that bookstore was still there.

From that day my daily routine became paint and walk, nothing else.

Late one humid afternoon the doorbell rang. It was Cecelia. "I thought you might be in the mood for a casserole." She set the covered basket down on the kitchen counter and began unpacking it. "It's a little early for dinner, I know." She eyed the empty wine bottle.

"Thank you, Cecelia, truly," I told her, putting on my best smile. "Dinner would be very nice."

She began laying out a nicely done meal and a beautifully arranged olive tray.

"Your father loved olives," she told me. "I assume you do too."

As we ate I told her about finding notes written by my father in various books.

"I know nothing about any notes in books," she said.

"But you probably read his book *The Elementary Language of the Heart*."

"Yes. In fact he read chapters of it to me as he was writing it."

I don't know why that put me off. I guess I felt Cece was intruding into my father's privacy, or maybe into my privacy. I hadn't enjoyed the book, but it was relatively autobiographical.

"Not a very good book," I said spitefully.

Cece shrugged. "It's a love story with a happy ending."

I sat there staring at the kitchen wall. "It's a fantasy. Although he put Achille, a man I used to know, into his book."

"I know who Achille is."

I stopped myself from telling her she had no idea who Achille really was.

I have the habit of skipping to the end of books, and I'd done that with *The Elementary Language of the Heart*. The ending was ambiguous. Did the hero fake his death and disappear, or did he really die?

"My father's death seemed so sudden. Did he end his own life?"

Cece said nothing. I got out a fresh bottle of Pinot noir and poured some for her.

"No, he didn't commit suicide," she said finally, taking a minute sip of wine. I watched her expression. Was she telling the truth?

"Or did he fake his own death and disappear to somewhere far away from here?" I went on. "The final accounting you gave me shows that he left some money in his own account in Monaco. Why would he do that?"

Cece shook her head, but did not smile at my speculation. "I don't know why he left money there," she said with finality. "You have legal access to his accounts, so you can move that money to your own account. I am quite sure he is dead."

Cece sat watching me eat. "I know he liked the thought of people disappearing from one life to make a new life somewhere else, but that's fiction, as in *Elementary Language*. That is not what happened here. He was quite ill, but he wanted to keep that to himself until very near the end. To spare you from a burden that you would not be able to do anything about. He said no final words to me. One day I came over for our daily brunch and found him dead in his bed."

"The immediate cremation, and clearing his room so quickly." I laid down my fork. "You could at least have phoned me."

"He said he wanted to spare you all that. He was very firm about that in his will. You have a copy. He wanted to simply disappear from life."

My anger rose. "Dammit! He should have talked to me about all that." I stopped myself before I started blaming her.

"It was his wish."

I drank half my glass of wine. "I can't help thinking pain medication must have clouded his judgment."

Cece's expression had hardened under my onslaught. "You resent me," she told me. "I understand your resentment. Stepmother antipathy, it's only natural."

"Please don't tell me how I feel," I snapped at her. "Especially not this superficial psychology..." I paused. "Sorry, I didn't mean to be so harsh."

"I know your father revealed a great deal of his life to you when you visited him in January," Cece said, which was not what I wanted to hear. My temper flared again.

"So you know about Lisa's scam and Eurovest threatening to investigate?"

Cecelia looked away. "Yes."

"Why didn't he tell me first?"

"Except for your last visit, when he was honest with you, too honest I think, he wanted all your visits to be pleasant ones. I think maybe you wanted that too. He kept the secret of your sister's...doings...from you until the end of his life. Do you think that is wrong? I don't."

"He decided to keep secrets from me for my own good," I snorted into my wine glass. "Rather condescending, don't you think?"

Cece leveled a look at me. She finished eating and set her nearly full wine glass aside. "He thought it best." She smiled. "I'm sure he told you that we all make the past what we want it to be. And we can make the present what we want it to be too."

"I suffered through years of guilt," I told Cece in a truculent tone. "Believing Lisa was speeding down an icy road to get my help. Now I am supposed to believe she was just trying to get out of Switzerland fast. I don't know if I feel less guilty or more guilty."

Cece looked at the floor. "Neither your father nor you could have saved her from a car crash on an icy road."

"Easy for you to say."

She gathered up her purse. "I'll go now."

I saw her to the door and watched her walk away down the sidewalk to her house.

I didn't know it then, but that was the last time I would ever see her.

Chapter 12

In August when I was circuiting the quadrangle on my daily walk, I noticed there were fresh-faced kids everywhere. Classes must be starting soon. My trek took me past the neo-Georgian façade of the College of Arts and Sciences. On impulse I went up the steps and inside. I found the art department at the end of the corridor. There was a small glass-walled gallery where a dozen examples of student art were on display.

"I'm just looking," I told the receptionist. Some of the student art was passable, all clearly beginner's work. I could identify every error, every attempt to emulate, and every attempt to be original.

At the receptionist's desk I asked for a brochure for the art department, and she handed me one. On the wall behind her was the department directory. There were two faculty vacancies.

I walked home enjoying the hot summer wind from the south. At home I poured myself a glass of Pinot and flipped through my completed paintings until I found the one I had done of Lisa.

You were so sharp-edged, over-confident and yet also young and unsure of yourself. You were only twenty years old, about the same age as those kids roaming the quadrangle. Yet you were already sophisticated, multilingual, cosmopolitan, very different from their midwestern naivete. And at the same time you were exactly like they are in their naivete.

I began to think of a future I might enjoy.

I was able to get an appointment with the dean of the College of Arts and Sciences on the basis of my father's name. The dean was gracious but evasive about my request for a position in the Arts Department. In turn I was gracious and evasive about my goals, though I was upfront with her about not having academic credentials or any interest in getting them. But I was not shy about bringing up my master's degree cum laude in art from NYU, my experience painting art that sold, and my experience managing Tempus and owning and operating Aeroptix Gallery in New York.

I'd never taught a class in my life, but I tried to express my belief that my own painting, my years of analyzing, buying, and selling art for galleries had given me insights that few teachers of art possess. I used my enthusiastic persona seasoned with the proper amount of earnestness and respect for the profession of teaching.

"Yes," the dean admitted after a time, "your background is quite impressive, and of course your father, when he was here, was certainly well respected."

I beamed at her. She glanced at my one-page CV (mostly true) on the desk in front of her. "We are pleased that someone with your...background...is interested in a position here. We do have openings. Your lack of advanced degrees is a point against you, but not an overwhelming obstacle." She smiled at me. "We value a passion for the subject and hard work as much as paper credentials."

She asked me to submit a formal application through their online system.

I told her I would do so immediately, thanked her with just the right touch of effusiveness, shook her hand, and went directly from her office to the administration building, where I located the office that handled bequests to the university. I arranged a transfer of $1,300,000 of my father's funds from his account in Monaco to endow a chair in his name at the university. And another $700,000 to fund an adjunct professorship in the Arts Department: me.

A week later I had my appointment as adjunct art professor, an office, a reserved parking place, control of one of the studios, and latitude to design my own classes. I moved my things into the office. The Arts dean had arranged a welcome tea for me, which I actually rather enjoyed. My colleagues accepted my presence without apparent rancor, which made sense—I was not on a tenure track, so I was no competition for them.

Back home, I poured myself a glass of Pinot and roamed the house, grinning.

"I think one fifty minute lecture course twice a week, and two sections of live-model figure study, each meeting once a week will be enough." I sat in a pleasant glow, imagining the enjoyment of talking about painting, getting back into a studio, and painting live models again.

My lecture course I grandly named Theory of Painting. I developed a syllabus, breaking the course into three consecutive courses. The university numbered them: Art 140 for the fall semester, Art 160 for the winter/spring semester, and Art 180 for the summer semester. Each would meet every Tuesday and Thursday from 9:40 to 10:30. The live-model painting courses were Beginning Figure Painting and Advanced Figure Painting, each a two-hour session.

I did feel a bit nervous walking from my car to my first class meeting. Yesterday I had come to campus and located my assigned classroom, and then found out it had been changed. I asked at the art department administration office, and the woman at the desk said it was because enrollment had been much greater than they had expected, so they'd moved my class to the auditorium at the end of the building.

The woman beamed at me. "Your class is very popular. Your name is known…"

"Well that's good." *But we'll see how many students sign up for the follow-on course, or drop out of this one,* I thought.

Students were still wandering into the auditorium when I walked onto the proscenium, plugged my laptop into the big-screen projector, and stepped behind the lectern. The big digital clock on the back wall of the auditorium said 9:40, time to start.

"I'm Sarah Kavan." There was a state-of-the-art audio system that kept a directional microphone aimed at me wherever I wandered, so I didn't have to mess with lapel microphones or a microphone on the lectern.

"The dean's office tells me many of you have heard of me and my artwork." I smiled at them, left the protection of the lectern, and walked to the front of the proscenium. "That's very gratifying. So to start off today, I'm going to show you my résumé. In pictures. You have the course outline, the assigned texts, and the weekly reading assignments in the online material. I'll discuss them briefly in a moment. You'll be graded on three things—a midterm exam, a final exam, and class participation."

A guy in the front row was fidgeting. I speared him with a look. Not unfriendly, but not encouraging. A look I'd perfected while dealing with an endless stream of artists in New York who wanted to show their work in my gallery.

"Most of the time I encourage questions and comments, but sometimes, like now, I want you to hold your questions until I go through some other stuff first, OK?"

He subsided.

I went through my paintings in roughly chronological order, starting with some student stuff my senior year. "OK," I said. "You've seen my résumé, now give me some comments and questions." Hands shot up all over the auditorium. "But you first." I pointed at the guy who'd wanted to say something before we started.

"The course outline says our primary text is *Art and Visual Perception* by Arnheim. That doesn't seem…"

"…doesn't seem like an art overview book? It isn't," I told him. "But let me paraphrase from the introduction to that book: 'Mere exposure to masterworks does not suffice…many people look at art books and visit museums without gaining access to art. The inborn ability to understand through the eyes has been put to sleep and must be reawakened.'"

He looked thoughtful. "Thank you, Doctor Kavan."

"Call me Sarah. I'm not a PhD."

Then I started taking questions and comments from the floor as fast as I could. They all had a similar subtext: What does it feel like to be a painter, how do I feel about this artist and that, about this type of art and that. But at their heart they were all asking the same things: What had it felt like to be a young and successful artist in New York City.

It was time for class to end, so I said, "We'll have to stop now, but we'll continue this discussion next time; in fact we'll continue it all semester, since you are getting to the central point of this class: What do things feel like, what do things look like."

The clock said exactly ten thirty. "But for today, we'll stop. See you next week." I turned off the electronics and closed my laptop briskly and strode off the proscenium.

I went home and poured myself a shot of Bushmills and toasted my reflection. It was exhilarating to talk about things I had been doing for more than ten years. In my painting days and in my gallery days I had talked about art a lot, but it was always from a business perspective. Now I was free to just talk about the elation of producing artwork—and the frustration.

I sipped the whiskey then poured it down the sink. I was not in the mood for something so strong. Instead, I made myself a cup of tea and sat in the reading chair by the living room window letting myself calm down. These kids had a lot of aspirations, and I felt energized to help them achieve all they could.

Teaching art came easily to me. I was talking about things I knew and loved to students who wanted to hear about it. What could be better?

From time to time one of the dean's lackeys would stop by "to see if I needed anything," but in fact to check up on me. I received a steady stream of invitations to various university events, which in fact were attempts to squeeze more money out of my father's estate through me. I'd successfully run a gallery in New York long enough to know how to evade that sort of charity-seeking, so soon the invitations stopped coming.

I'd always been an organized person, so I did not find it hard to organize and present the classroom material. I had thought student interaction would be stressful and disagreeable, but I found it was actually the best part of teaching. The students were bright, cheerful, eager to be in my class, and eager to participate. One or two even had a modicum of talent.

The assessments were the worst part: trying to put down a measure of teaching effectiveness and student progress. Very tough to do. I sympathized with the administration on that, though I would never tell them so. Any business has to have some sort of metrics to measure progress, or else you're just playing at running a business. And a university is a business, although its products—educated people and useful research—do not lend themselves to quantitative measures of success. Fortunately for me, undergraduate classroom courses like mine rely entirely on grades, which makes it easier. For my figure painting classes I devised a metric I'd learned from my father's economics book about metrics developed for areas with "soft quants." My associate dean was quite impressed, and afterward left me alone to grade as I pleased.

My studio sessions were wonderful compared to New York. No longer did I have to worry about getting models, paying them, and arranging for space with good light (which is very expensive in New York). Both the beginning and advanced figure painting classes were full from the first day. I guess I did have some sort of reputation as a painter. And I was thrilled that the students were genuinely interested in learning.

Fall semester ended and, after a quiet holiday, winter/spring semester began. My lecture course, Art 160, was full. I guess my students in Art 140 had been suitably impressed with my stories.

I used the Arnheim text again, but added a list of standard texts and gallery inventories as references. In class I told stories. Stories about artists, various aspects of painting, or styles, or an era, or the economics of buying and selling art. I found I was a born storyteller just like my father.

I took great poetic license with details of the lives of painters I talked about. My intent was to interest the students in the artist and his work, and I believe I was able to do that.

The students were enthusiastic, energetic, and enjoyably naive. And I knew more than I thought I did about many of the painters of the past and the present.

The days flew by.

But one day in March I was caught off balance. It was during my Art 160 lecture class. I always insisted that my students ask questions, not just of me but of each other. My first semester I had been surprised by how personal some of their questions for me were. I don't believe they were being intentionally impolite, but they knew I had been a practicing artist, and they wanted to know about my experiences.

As soon as I reached the proscenium a hand went up at the back of the auditorium.

"How did you become interested in being a painter?"

That was a question I was not prepared for. "It is, was, an interest of mine since high school. My mother enjoyed going to art galleries, and I used to accompany her, and slowly I began to appreciate what powerful emotions a painting could generate. I learned to see the world as images that told stories or created emotion. And at some point I wanted to learn to put those images on canvas."

I babbled on about looking at art books, but the students, sensing that I was just generalizing, were losing interest. I moved the discussion to another topic.

Later that evening after three glasses of Pinot, I found myself pacing the house, muttering, "Why did I become a painter?" I had never discussed it with anyone, just applied to NYU Art School and left for New York as soon as I was accepted.

But there had been an influence, a triggering event, back in my almost forgotten high school days. The influence had not been a course. I took no art classes at St. Pete High.

It had been the silent, dusty book shelves of Haslam's Used Books. The used bookstore had been my refuge from the cold emptiness of my mother's house and the polite distance between my mother and me that neither she nor I could, or would, break. I'd bought many books there, but it had been the art books that had set me on my life's path. And my trips to the art museum with Mother. Visits full of silences. She never talked about art much. And she seldom bought paintings, but she had loved a particular Joan Miró. My father had bought it for her. My father had kept it when he sold the house in Florida. I went into the hallway and stared at that modest Joan Miró painting. Something my mother had loved. *I can no longer clearly remember Mother's face. I remember only photos of her, not the reality of her. She is becoming ghostly.*

I woke in the night. The clock said one thirty. I got up and flipped through my old paintings and found the one I was looking for. It was the only painting I had ever done of my mother. She was dressed in white, her face turned away from the viewer, staring out the picture window of her house in Florida. Staring at a manicured lawn on a neat suburban street. Lawn sprinklers create tiny rainbows. The sky is clear blue.

I set the painting on the kitchen counter. In the harsh fluorescent light, it still kept its air of ghostliness, Mother's features faintly reflected in the window glass. *This is all I have left of you, Mother, just a reflection of someone thinking thoughts I will never know. I don't want to forget you, but it is happening.* I took a photo of the painting, put it back in the stack, and returned to bed.

Next session I put the photo of my painting of my mother up on the screen for the class to see. The back of her head, her white dress, and the manicured lawn and pastel houses outside the window are what you see first. It takes a moment for the reflection of the woman's face in the glass to register. Her expression is ambiguous.

"Last session one of you asked a question I didn't answer well. It's an important question, so I'll try again to answer it. Where did my interest in art come from?" I paused. "For me, it came from my mother. I didn't realize it at the time, but because of her I learned to see the world in images. Images with meaning. This is a portrait I did of her."

"Is it easy or difficult to paint someone you know?"

"Both. It is easy to paint your first impression of someone. But if you try to paint someone you know quite well, it becomes harder." I turned a threatening glare on the students. "But don't just make a photo with your paints. Photography and painting are two separate arts."

"So, it must take you a long time to get the painting right," said the persistent guy with the worst-looking red hair I'd ever seen. He usually had a comment—or five—every class. But, to be fair, some of his comments were to the point.

I faced the painting on the screen, then the students. "I painted this one in about three hours."

There was a ripple of comments around the room.

"Three hours? That's amazing." The girl in the front row with the bleached blonde hair was wide-eyed.

"Sometimes a painting will take days or weeks. But for me, once an image has formed in my mind, it usually goes onto the canvas relatively quickly. Although sometimes you just get stuck. If you do, it is better to put that canvas aside and work on another one for a while. If you keep struggling with a painting, you generally make it worse, not better."

I tacked an end on the topic. "I became a painter because of my mother. She had an interest in art that I absorbed without really noticing."

"Your mother was interested in art, but not a painter," a fresh-faced girl in the third row commented skeptically, and a bit sarcastically.

"That's right," I said, looking up at the screen where my mother continued to stare out at the bright green lawn. "She never expressed any interest in becoming a painter."

The grass was green and the daffodils in full bloom, but the day was cold, overcast, and windy. I thought about chiaroscuro. I started some water boiling, got out the little Noritake tea set that had been my mother's and some Harney & Sons Earl Grey tea.

I sat in the living room in my father's old chair savoring the tea. A feeling arose in me—the need to paint. I was already painting twice a week at the university studio in my figure painting class, but that was simply little bits of painting to illustrate how I might capture a feature of human anatomy.

What I was feeling again, for the first time in a long time, was the need to put full images on canvas. All my materials were still in their crates in the garage. It was time to get them out and get back to work.

I opened the door to my father's bare bedroom, went inside, and stood looking north through the sheers at the backyard. Although I had come into this room many times and stood trying to gather the essence of who he had been, of who he and I had been to each other, the room continued to be just empty space. He was gone.

I stood at the window. The wind rippled the grass in the backyard.

"So," I said, "this room is now my studio."

It didn't take long to set up. My completed canvases went from the guest bedroom closet into his old closet. As I moved them I realized how unfamiliar they now seemed. They were uniformly large, slashes of scarlet, burnt sienna, Prussian blue—faces and figures of strangers from New York sidewalks and subways or from my imagination, glaring or squinting or crying. I saw no smiles. Tenebristic images of unhappy, preoccupied people caught in some moment of angst.

The last painting I stacked in the closet was the portrait I'd done of Lisa. The technique was good; I had captured the Lisa I thought I knew; but now I knew her better.

Her portrait was one of the last paintings I had done in that very dark and edgy style.

By the end of the winter/spring semester I had half a dozen new canvases done. I'd contacted Ellis in New York to ask if I could send him some photos to see if he'd be willing to show them. He refused politely, saying he was overstocked with paintings at the moment. Check with him in six months.

In all my free time I painted with the same focus I had once had in New York, but now with less anger in the brush strokes. My paintings were good but not inspired. But I remained confident I would regain my old mastery, then the images would flow onto canvas almost with a life of their own. I had to work at it, but my brush techniques had improved.

Sometimes I felt lonely and sorry for myself. I had many acquaintances, mostly university people, but no real friends. I never invited anyone to my house, and aside from a few perfunctory welcome-to-the-university parties early on, I had never been invited to anyone else's house.

Chapter 13

A cold rain in June. I drank coffee and sat looking out the kitchen window. This kind of weather always gave me a cozy feeling of being inside, warm, and safe. I could stay home, drink tea, read a good book.

"But not today." I rinsed my coffee cup and gathered up my laptop. "Today is a fast overview of contemporary artists." I'd included some slides of my own early work from 1993 in New York when success first came my way.

As I pulled out of my driveway my eye registered a bit of blue-and-red color on the lawn of a house down the block. A realtor's sign.

I expected a low turnout in my class because of the cold and rain, but the auditorium was full to overflowing.

"A lot of people apparently need someplace to get in out of the weather," I told the class as I got my presentation running on the big screen behind me. I stood on the proscenium and put the first slide on the screen, which was a photo of the crowd in Tempus Gallery on a cold night in October, my art on display. In fact my first big showing since I'd graduated from NYU. The gallery was packed, people dressed in New York's style of the moment—women with scarlet mouths wearing black leather, men in black tie, kids in grunge. Champagne glasses and cigarette smoke.

"What do you think is happening here?" I asked the crowd and students jumped in with half a dozen guesses.

"Free champagne?"

"Free money, you mean…"

"Somebody just got paroled. It looks like a prison crowd to me…"

"Somebody celebrating finding an apartment in New York…"

"No, somebody celebrating leaving New York."

"How do you know it's New York?" I asked. "It is, but how did you know, or was that a lucky guess?"

"It has that sense," a girl with brilliant red hair said tentatively.

"The clothes…" somebody in the back said.

"Back to your point." I pointed at the girl with red hair. "Could you paint that sense?"

They quieted.

"That's what I want you to think about when you are composing a painting in your head. Before you mix your first color. What is the sense you wish to display to the viewer? You may want multiple senses, several people, each different, the setting ambiguous perhaps, but show me the emotion when you paint."

We talked about this for a moment; I got some good feedback. Then somebody said, "So, in this slide you're showing us, what is happening? What is the sense?"

"I was there." I put the laser pointer's red dot on a person in the crowd. "That's me. It was the opening of a new exhibition at a gallery in Manhattan many years ago. I had just sold my first painting. My first serious painting." I moved the laser to a painting on the gallery wall, but it was angled to the point the image was indecipherable.

"You must have been ecstatic," said a gawky guy with curly blonde hair, always looking like he'd just gotten out of bed five minutes ago.

"I was ecstatic," I told them. "And after a while, apprehensive. I'd made my first sale, now the hard work starts: making the second sale and the third…"

I concluded my lecture with a montage of my own early work.

"How much of it sold?"

"All of it."

I pointed with the laser pointer. "This one is now in MOMA."

"You have a painting in MOMA?" a girl in the second row gasped, like someone in a Victorian novel.

"In the Annex, yes," I told her. "But don't be too impressed. It's a minor work. It is expressive of my style at the time. But your success as a painter does not depend on getting paintings into big collections. It's a cliché, I know—'paint what's in your heart, not what's popular'—but it's true. As I've mentioned before, there are three aspects to train yourself in: heart, hand, eye. Take what's in your heart and put it on canvas. But be willing to learn from others. Don't paint something because you think it's trendy, or that it will sell. Even if it does, you're not going to feel that good about it later. There are a lot of second-rate paintings around. Don't make more of them, OK?"

I turned off the screen behind me and brought the lights up in the auditorium. "Don't take fame too seriously. It comes and goes, and if you get addicted to it, when it goes it can destroy you. That first big sale is an important milestone, worth celebrating. But it is also the signal that you need to work harder than ever to be the best painter you can be. Live up to expectations. Your own, especially. See you next class."

After the auditorium had cleared, I put my first slide back up. That night in New York when I'd sold my first big, serious painting. I remembered that day, and night, with clarity. But I could no longer clearly see who I was now. I knew only that I had changed from the twenty-three-year-old me selling her first painting.

After a while I gathered up my things, turned the lights off in the auditorium, and drove home. It was cold, colder than that morning, but the rain had stopped.

In the kitchen I poured my customary glass of Pinot and stood sipping it, my coat still on. It had been a good day, a good class. And my recollection of New York and Milan and Achille, all the excitement of those days, felt good. Good to remember the good times.

I was staring through the kitchen window when I realized the *House for Sale* sign was in Cece's front lawn. I phoned the number on the sign, and a woman answered, "Remax Realty."

"The house you're advertising at 1350 Thilly Avenue, how long has it been on the market?"

"Just a week. But if you are interested, you should make an offer soon. We've had a lot of interest in it. Properties that close to campus always turn over quickly."

"I'm a neighbor. I'd like to get back in touch with the woman who owns that house…do you have a contact phone number?"

After a minute's delay she quoted me a phone number. "That's the daughter's number," the realtor said. "They live in Dunedin, Florida. Very sad about her mother. Suffered a stroke a month ago. They took her to an assisted living facility near them in Florida…."

After the phone call, I roamed the house, wine glass in hand, once again cursing myself for distancing myself from people and losing friendships over my own irritability.

I stood in front of my father's bookcase. Often the books would fall open to a certain page, and Durrell's *Clea* was no exception.

"I am…serene and happy, a real human being, an artist at last."

But I am not.

Deep summer. Hot humid days; I wait until dusk to take my daily walk.

I have my health, money in the bank, a job I enjoy. "And I have art," I said aloud. A couple of girls walking by eyed me, no doubt reconfirming to themselves that all university professors eventually lose touch with reality and roam the campus talking to themselves.

At home I told the black glass of the microwave, "I have more than art, I also have my students. And maybe, just maybe, I am making a small change for the better in their lives."

The air conditioner hummed smoothly, reminding me of my mother's house as she lay dying.

Chapter 14

My enthusiasm for teaching art came in part from the stories I told my students. I gave myself great latitude in interpreting the lives of artists from the past. Storytelling makes history come alive, and that was my primary objective: create enthusiasm for great art in the minds of my students.

I estimated that about 5 percent had enough talent to succeed, and that only a handful of that 5 percent would have enough drive to actually sell paintings.

Even though I was only an adjunct professor, I still was assigned to various committees. But not being on a tenure track, most committee assignments I simply ignored. What would they do, deny me tenure?

But I'd decided to participate on the Strategic Planning Committee for the College of Arts and Sciences. Maybe I could actually contribute something. The first few meetings were deadly dull and useless. It wasn't until the November meeting that I really became aware of Kevin.

He was the only other member of the committee younger than seventy. A smart, quiet guy, he said little in the meetings. He had nice features—he wasn't tall, but had a loping walk that at first I thought was kind of funny but lately was beginning to think rather charming.

When the meeting broke up and we were all going out the door into the November dusk, Kevin invited me to have coffee with him.

"How about a glass of wine instead?" I asked.

"There's a student hangout on Ninth Street, German-themed, but who knows, might be good." He laughed, which made him look even younger.

"I know it," I told him. "The wine there is mediocre, but it's cheap. And it's nearby. Let's go."

At the Rathskeller, we got a booth (painted plywood, the height of style) and each ordered a glass of Cabernet Sauvignon, which the server brought us with lightning speed. She knew that old geezers like us would be good for a better tip than the college students at the other booths.

Kevin and I commiserated about the Strategic Planning Committee. "Goals should be short, achievable, and have metrics," Kevin said.

"And there shouldn't be too many of them," I said. "What's his name, the committee chair? Thorenson? He wants twenty goals on the strategic plan."

"Ridiculous, I agree," Kevin said. Toasting stupidity, we raised our glasses. "But he will never change."

I waved my hand at the kids at the tables. "They think we're so old we have stopped changing too. Maybe they are right."

Kevin grinned. "Well, let me amend my statement that Thorenson—Sorenson, whatever his name is—will change. But he will change very slowly, because he doesn't want to change. I think we all change throughout our lives. I think it's impossible not to change." He laughed.

I smiled. "That's something my father might have said."

Kevin sipped his Cab. "Not as bad as I expected." He studied the tabletop for a moment. "Do you mind if I ask you if you've been married?"

I bristled a little, then reminded myself that I was the new me—more confident, more open, more trusting. "Not married, but heavily involved for a time. Long ago. And you?"

"Married once, no kids, divorced after eight years."

"Interested in kids?"

"No."

"That was succinct."

"On that point I am very succinct. I've known since I was a young man that I had no interest in children. Being a professor, which, by the way, I happen to enjoy, unlike the rest of the deadheads around the conference table this afternoon—" We both laughed. "Provides the outlet for any paternal feelings I may have. I am passionate about my specialty, eighteenth-century English literature, and I enjoy discussing it with my students. I like the energy and the...openness to new ideas they bring, but at the end of the day I go to my home and they go to their homes."

I nodded. "I feel the same way. As you know, my background is not in academia, so I was expecting the teaching and paper reading to be the worst part of the job. Instead, I find it is the best part."

He nodded. His grin always seemed wry. One side of his mouth turned down; the other side turned up. But I was finding it attractive.

I waved at the waiter for another glass of wine, but Kevin waved the waiter away. "Come with me to my place. I have lots of good wine."

"And lustful intentions?"

He grinned. "Perhaps."

I said more seriously, "I like being with you, but let's don't rush things, OK?"

"I agree. In fact, I insist we don't rush."

His house was only two blocks from my house. Beautifully refinished inside, the old wood trim glowing with dark walnut color, the house had wall-to-wall carpet, fairly new. The kitchen looked tiny. He showed me what looked like a glass-faced double refrigerator that took up a third of one wall of the kitchen.

"So this is what a wine cellar looks like," I said. No wonder the kitchen seemed small. He'd had this alcove built to house the specialty refrigerator. "I know very little about wine," I told him, "even though I drink a lot of it. But I am impressed. Must be several hundred bottles of wine here."

"About four hundred at the moment. Though there is an estate sale this weekend that I plan to attend, so I may buy a dozen more."

Kevin took a bottle of Argo Pinot noir and poured us each a bit in a large glass.

We sat in the living room, him on the chair, me on the sofa.

"Am I supposed to be sipping this?" I asked, displaying my half-empty glass.

Kevin hopped up and got the bottle and topped my glass up. "No, not at all; drink at your normal pace. I'm not such a wine snob that I insist everyone drink in certain ways, although I have acquaintances who would insist on it." He laughed. "I love all kinds of wine, but I try not to be a wine snob," he finished dryly. Then he brightened. "I knew your father, slightly. He was still on the faculty when I first came here. Quite an impressive man in person. I always felt a bit intimidated around him, though he was always affable enough. He seemed to have a reserve—not haughtiness, just an immense force of knowledge. Brilliance, I guess you could say. There was a rumor that he'd been considered for a Nobel in economics."

"That's true. He was briefly considered, but did not make the preliminary selection. His nomination occurred just at the wrong time for him. My younger sister died in a car crash right about then. It was an emotionally bad time, for all of us. He left his position…I'm babbling, sorry."

"No, not at all." Kevin poured a minute quantity of the Pinot into his glass and said, "The University of Missouri was very fortunate to have him for a few years. I assume he…passed away?"

"Yes, a year ago."

Kevin nodded. The wine really was excellent. We talked for a while about inconsequential things. Then I told him it was time for me to go home.

He walked me to the door. "I won't kiss you, not because you're not kissable, and not because I don't want to, but because we agreed we would proceed slowly. Is that OK? Or am I explaining too much?"

"You aren't explaining too much. We need to be as open as possible with each other," I told him. But then he stepped forward and gave me a quick hug I wasn't expecting. "How about dinner tomorrow? Or am I going too fast?"

I smiled. "Dinner tomorrow will be fine."

"I'll see you tomorrow then." He waved as I drove off.

The Sorrento restaurant was nicely appointed. The music was Italian, but neither smarmy '50s nor high-concept opera, something subtler. And best of all, I found I could have spinach substituted for the pasta under filet of sole.

"I'm nearly finished with my paper on Maria Edgeworth," Kevin said. He swirled his Merlot reflectively. "I think it will bring something substantial to the study of the eighteenth-century English novel. The long eighteenth century."

My eyebrows went up.

"Sorry. Jargon. Academics tend to consider literature from 1660 through 1830 as a single era in literature, though evolving quickly."

"Interesting," I said. "Given everything going on in Britain during that period—industrial revolution, rise of the British Empire, Napoleonic wars…I assume the major writers of the period had those things centered in their stories?"

"Surprisingly to most modern readers, no. Austen, for example, never mentions the wars and hardly touches on the Empire, even though two of her brothers were in the navy."

"She died young, didn't she?"

"Yes," he said in a somber tone. I had to suppress a smile at his suddenly grave look, as though one of his own relatives had recently died. "She was only forty-one when she died." Kevin brightened. "On the other hand, Maria Edgeworth lived to be seventy-three, and Frances Burney, another writer of the period, lived to eighty. Rather tragic, Burney's last years. She outlived her parents, all her siblings, her husband, and her son, who died at age forty-three. Rather lonely, I suspect."

I tried to turn the thought out of my mind, but it echoed back: *I am the last of my family. I am alone.*

"Am I boring you?" Kevin asked.

I reached out and touched his hand. "Not at all. I was just reflecting on what you said about Frances Burney. I've outlived all my family too."

He smiled. "I won't ask you about your family…too presumptuous. I know only your father's reputation." He ducked his head. "And yours."

"Mine?" I downed my wine and Kevin smoothly replenished my glass before the waiter could. "The course catalog advertises you as one of the brightest young New York painters of the 1990s."

I chuckled. "I guess I'm flattered. That was a long time ago. I was never very well-known outside of New York, but I was able, through luck and talent, to start selling paintings right out of art school. I was very, very fortunate in that."

He smiled becomingly. "You seem to have weathered the rigors of minor fame quite well."

I laughed. "My fame was small enough that I could easily handle the lack of it."

The evening was pleasant and leisurely—good food and excellent wine. At my house he walked me to my door. I didn't dodge his kiss, but returned it softly, not too short, not too long.

"Can I see you again?" he asked.

"Yes. But we agreed to proceed slowly, OK?"

He nodded. "Certainly," he said, and then waved as he returned to his car.

Inside, I poured myself a glass of wine and toasted my new friendship. "Here's to you Kevin. Or maybe I say, here's to us."

Kevin came by Saturday to pick me up. It was a typical November day in the Midwest—blustery, cold, and overcast. "The forecast said sun today, and I was thinking of a picnic, champagne, and a lake view, but it's too cold. Why don't we have our picnic at my house. I have a working fireplace and plenty of split firewood."

It was delightful. The afternoon passed swiftly as we ate our snacks and drank the champagne, then a bottle of Cabernet Sauvignon. Evening came early.

At one point I mentioned rather shamefacedly, " I tried reading the book you were talking about the other day, *Belinda*, but I quit after thirty pages.

He smiled. "Eighteenth- and nineteenth-century English fiction is an acquired taste."

"I did like the depiction of Madame Delacour's empty life."

"If you had told me you loved it, I would have been quite skeptical that you'd actually read it. My students do that all the time in my classes—read a summary, then try to impress me with their knowledge. I not only know the book very well, but I also know most of the available summaries well enough to know which summary they are relying on."

I laughed.

"People have different tastes in reading." He frowned. "I regret to say that many of my colleagues in the English department don't have that opinion. Most of them insist there is only one great literature, their own specialty, and everything else is tripe."

"Same in the visual arts," I said. "Art's purpose is to entertain and inspire, nothing more. Many kinds of art appeal to many kinds of people."

Despite the occasional missteps in our conversation, the afternoon and evening were wonderful. He made a light dinner for us. Outside was cold and a wind had come up, so, without either of us saying it, I decided to spend the night with him. It went well, despite the fact that we were both clearly out of practice having sex.

The next morning he made some great coffee, unlike my whatever-coffee-is-on-sale sort, and we sat in silence for a time watching the clouds racing by. The overcast was breaking up. The wind was cold, but it would be sunny soon.

After a while, we ate a light breakfast, and I told him, "I'll be on my way now. I had a great time. Soon the light will be good for painting, which is what I plan to do today."

He picked up his keys and was about to go for our coats, and I said, "Just my coat, please. I'd rather walk home. It's not far."

We kissed, and I stepped out the door.

And I did get some painting done that day. And I saw Kevin the next weekend and the next.

I learned to read again.

Many of the books on the shelf were books my father had brought from Mother's house in Florida after she'd died. Many of them had been mine—used paperbacks from Haslam's used bookstore, long forgotten. But now as I reread them, I remembered them fondly.

My own painting was improving. I still favored deep chiaroscuro, but the faces and forms of the models in class at the university brought a lightness and depth to my paintings. My faces and figures looked far more human than the images of distraught strangers that inhabit the paintings I did in New York.

Chapter 15

T he day before Thanksgiving break is usually a low attendance day. I walked into the amphitheater classroom expecting to find only a handful of students, but all eighty seats were taken. I loved teaching art to students with this kind of enthusiasm. And discussions of de La Tour and his followers were always among my favorite topics. That was today's topic.

"It's easy to find the light in these paintings." I put de La Tour's *Magdalene with the Smoking Flame* on screen. "But think about how even with this stark contrast, how the Magdalene is formed by both the light and the darkness. We can only see the side of her face, but we know her expression. Her posture tells us something, and the darkness behind her is what forms her posture. The light also affects the perspective. Said another way, it is best to choose your painting's viewpoint perspective and the position of your light source at the same time. Now let me hear from you."

I'd asked each student to write a paragraph comparing de La Tour and Caravaggio's use of chiaroscuro and be prepared to present it to the entire class. I chose a student at random and asked them to summarize their findings, then another student, and another, then I asked for input from everyone. The presentations were better than I expected, both in content and in delivery, and the follow-up discussion was spirited. Finally, on time at ten thirty, I shouted, "OK, that's enough. Put your mid-term assignments in a stack on the table by the door and go home and eat turkey. See you after Thanksgiving break!" They piled their folders on the table as they pushed out of the auditorium.

I put all the folders in a cardboard box I'd brought and was about to turn the lights off and leave, when on impulse I put de La Tour's painting back up on the screen. I turned the auditorium lights off. The painting was striking.

Am I like that? Defined by darkness.

"Nonsense!" I snapped. I turned off the screen, closed my laptop, and hauled the box of student papers and my laptop to my car.

Columbia was besieged with cold wind and cloudy skies. I longed to be sitting in front of Kevin's fireplace, but Kevin and I had uncharacteristically decided to spend Saturday night in our separate houses. I had midterms I wanted to start grading right away. I knew if I didn't start immediately I would put it off until the night before classes started again, and my comments would be superficial.

I was working my way through the folders of my students in my Art 140 class. I'd asked them to provide me four of their own paintings that they felt were their best work, and a paragraph for each telling me why these four were good, using the analytical concepts we'd discussed in class. There were eighty students in the class, and Kevin had warned me against assigning many essay assignments since the time required to grade them would be horrendous. But we were halfway through the semester, and I'd covered all the principles I wanted to cover. Now I wanted to make sure the students were not only retaining the principles; I wanted to see whether they could apply these principles to their own work.

I quickly went through all eighty folders and separated them into two piles. One pile was the students with little or no aptitude. That was about sixty of the eighty. Then I went through all eighty folders again, reading the four paragraphs in each. I put a checkmark on the front of the folders of those students who showed good comprehension of the principles I'd talked about. I had to laugh at some of the less-informed comments. Some students apparently had no idea what I'd been talking about the last six weeks.

In the small pile of twenty folders, eight had checkmarks. I'd review and comment on them first.

I went to the kitchen and started to open a bottle of wine, but instead phoned Kevin. "It's noon. Unless you've already eaten, why don't you come on over and make us lunch?"

He laughed. "I'll be there in twenty minutes."

He came in and gave me a hug and a kiss, his face cold from the wind. "Looks like it might rain later today."

He made a terrific lunch out of leftovers, then we sat on the couch watching the wind whip the treetops over the backyard. I opened a bottle of Argo Pinot noir, poured two glasses, and brought them out. He raised his eyebrows at the wine, but then raised his glass in a toast. "To winter. My favorite season."

The wine was dark and flavorful.

We sat for a while, then I took his hand and led him down the corridor to my studio. "Let me show you a painting I did several years ago." I opened the drapes on the cloudy day outside, slid the closet door open, and flipped through my old paintings until I found the one I was looking for. I set it against the closet door, turned on the room lights, and let Kevin study it.

He squatted down and had a close look, then backed away and leaned against the window ledge. "I don't know much about art," he said to me.

I shrugged at him. "I know."

He turned his attention back to the portrait. "You look determined in this painting. Angry, uncertain, and condescending—sorry I sound so negative. The painting itself is striking. The dramatic brush strokes…"

"That's a palette knife."

"…and the deep darkness behind you. Is that a shadowy figure I see in the background?"

"I think so, but I'm not sure. These images come out of a part of my mind that I don't know very well myself."

He raised his eyebrows. "I've seen your recent work. This is very different. Assertive, negative, but at the same time very…confused…lost. I don't mean to sound so critical."

"You don't need to apologize. It is a very dark piece, from a rather dark time of my life. I painted it just before my sister died. Perhaps I had a premonition of disaster." I put it back in the closet and we returned to the fireplace in the living room. "The face in the painting is not me. It is my sister Lisa. That's a painting I did of her when she was twenty. She'd come to visit me in New York, just before she got killed in a car accident." I looked at my empty wine glass. "The visit was not a happy one. We could never quite seem to drop our pretenses and be friends." I twirled my glass. "It was the last time I ever saw her." Tears filled my eyes.

Kevin took my glass and set it aside and kissed me. "Maybe it's time to stop being so hard on yourself." He changed the subject. "I see you did not take my advice about minimizing your students' homework assignment. He nodded toward the pile of student mid-term folders.

"Well, of all eighty, there are eight that show real understanding of the coursework and have a talent for painting. I'll write comments on them first, in detail. Then some fairly generic remarks for the rest."

Kevin picked up a folder from the short pile and took it to the kitchen. "This is a painting of you."

I went to the kitchen and looked. There was a resemblance. Perhaps the student had done the painting in my live-model class, using my face instead of the model, but that was not the case. The painting was of two people sitting on a low stone wall, half turned toward each other. They were smiling, but thoughtful. There was no background, just formless pale white, a Vermeer sky.

I took it from him and studied it a moment. I was finally seeing myself in the woman in the painting— it's strange how we often don't know how we look to others. The man she was with… "Oh!" I sucked in air. "I know that man!" I pointed. "That is Achille, a guy I used to date."

"Then no wonder that woman is you," Kevin said. "Who painted this?"

I got the name sheets out and went down to number 42. "Mariangela Gianinni." My heart was pounding. "That's Achille's last name, Gianinni."

We looked at each other and both spoke at the same time. "His daughter."

"Here in Missouri, in my art class?"

"You look like you need a drink," Kevin said and poured us each another glass of wine. It occurred to me that I hadn't had a drink of whiskey in a year. And I'd given up cigarettes long before that.

Kevin studied his glass. "I would toast to winter again," he said slowly, "but I want to hear from you first—how will you deal with having Mariangela in your class?"

"I'll treat her like any other student. Well, like one of my best students." I closed her folder. "She has talent."

"I meant about the past?"

"The past is past," I said. "I…"

My phone chimed a text alert. *This is Mari Gianinni, one of your students.*

I was shocked. "It's Mariangela texting me! I said.

She rang my phone, and I picked it up.

"I must go to London," Mariangela said. "I need your help. I am sorry. I must…" She began crying.

"Where are you now?" I asked.

She said she was at the bus station waiting for a bus to the airport. "I need to go to the airport now. I must return to London immediately. But there is no bus until tonight. The buses have gone; they were full…" She started crying again. "I wanted to ask you if you knew of any other way I can get to the airport. I am sorry to bother you, but you are the only person I know…"

"We can drive you to the airport," I told her. Kevin raised his eyebrows. But after I clicked the phone off and told him we needed to leave right now to drive Mariangela to the airport, he just gave me that wry grin of his, then pulled on his coat and off we went.

Mari was at the front door the bus station, suitcase at her feet. She had a red beret in her hands and was wearing a blue-black trench coat, jeans, and leather boots. Kevin put her suitcase in the trunk, she climbed in the back seat, and we started for the airport.

As we drove, I helped her get a reservation by phone on an afternoon flight from St. Louis that would get her to New York in time to connect with a nine p.m. flight departing for Heathrow.

"Are you Achille Gianinni's daughter? Achille who lived in Milan, who is a stock trader..." I babbled.

"Yes." She dabbed at her tears. "My father. He knew you." Then she fell silent. I heard her crying softly.

Mariangela has been in my Art 140 class this semester, and I didn't even notice.

After a while I said, "After you...do what you need to do in London...I hope you will return and continue with your art studies here in Missouri."

"Yes, yes, I want to continue. Very much."

"Mariangela. A very beautiful name," Kevin said, trying to lighten the tension.

"My father named me after an actress whose movies he liked," Mari said, blushing. "Mariangela

Melato. I'm told I look a little bit like her." She was silent for a few miles. Then she said softly, "My father told me I should study with you. He also told me that you knew how art is bought and sold, what art is good and what is not so good, which is as important as knowing how to paint if one intends to be a real artist. He had great affection for you." She blushed again and looked away. "Love, I think." She began to cry softly again. "My father has been ill for a long time. Cancer. He just died. I must return to London…" She broke down in sobs.

I felt my heart go numb. Achille dead. Tears began pouring down my cheeks and would not stop. Achille and me in Milan, our ski trip to Zermatt, Achille and me in the swimming pool at Villa Fiore. The night air cold, the mountain peaks sharp in starlight, but the water warm and the blue lights were pale enough we could see the stars overhead. I would float on my back, admiring Auriga and Orion, then swim down to the bottom of the pool and let myself drift to the surface. Veuve Clicquot and red roses inside. The bedroom warm. All of Villa Fiore was done in shades of red and white. Achille, who had listened to me while I told him all the angst within me—of my father, my sister, my mother, my paintings, New York.

We got to the airport, parked the car, and Mari and I composed ourselves. The three of us walked to the line to go through security. I hugged her. "I am so sorry. When you have had time…and your mother is OK, come back to Missouri. Please."

"I will," she said. We were both crying. Even Kevin's eyes were wet.

We watched for a while as the line advanced and Mari passed through security. Then we started back to the parking garage.

"I hope she comes back to Missouri," I said, my voice uneven.

"I think she will," Kevin said. "She thinks a lot of you." He put his arm around me as we walked down the concourse to the parking garage. "I think a lot of you too, Sarah."

We got to the car, and Kevin let it warm up for a minute. "I think you may have found your little sister," he told me.

He shifted into gear but then put it back in park and leaned over and kissed me and whispered, "I love you, Sarah."

"I love you too, Kevin."